Swerve

Swerve

Swerve

Michelle McGriff

URBAN
Renaissance

www.urbanbooks.net

Urban Books, LLC
78 East Industry Court
Deer Park, NY 11729

ISBN 13: 978-1-60162-232-7
ISBN 10: 1-60162-232-5

First Printing December 2010
Printed in the United States of America

10 9 8 7 6 5 4 3 2 1

Distributed by Kensington Publishing Corp.
Submit Wholesale Orders to:
Kensington Publishing Corp.
C/O Penguin Group (USA) Inc.
Attention: Order Processing
405 Murray Hill Parkway
East Rutherford, NJ 07073-2316
Phone: 1-800-526-0275
Fax: 1-800-227-9604

SWERVE
. . . an unexpected turn of events.
By Michelle McGriff

Acknowledgments

Writing is an action word. As writers, we should be constantly moving, advancing, growing. As a growing writer, stretching is what we do best. We reach out past comfort zones and commercial norms to find new and exciting stories to deliver to readers. In doing that, we only hope that our readers are ready to receive, what we feel, is a gift to them.

Swerve is such a gift. It's new and fresh and hopefully leading to a new turn in my writing. Throwing together my love of edgy romance (meaning: on the edge of not being romantic, haha) with a little suspense, I have now added a bit more "outside the norm" topics. I am by no means crossing into the paranormal genre with the story. I would say that it's closer to fantasy or sci-fi. Yet, it's got a realistic story line with characters who show up from my previous works. This story again attempts to answer my ongoing writing question: "What if?"

In order to see this story to completion, I again called on my friends for support, and I would like to thank them here. I would like to thank national bestselling author Shelia M. Goss for always being there for support and sisterly love. It's your insomnia that has kept me going strong, even across the time zones. To new author Jennifer Coissiere, for sharing her excitement over the process with me. It's new writers like this who keep me reminded of why I'm doing this. It's for the love.

Speaking of love, I want to always thank those I love: my friends, my family, and the one man who is all that

Acknowledgments

rolled up into one. He is my muse, my counterpart, and the smile I wear each day. I'd say he's what keeps me writing but that wouldn't be true. Maxine Thompson keeps me writing. Thank you for cracking the whip! Thank you, Carl Weber, for publishing my books; I hope you continue to grow as a company so that we can continue to grow our audience. Thank you, Natalie Weber, for your choice in editors; my books never looked and read so good.

Thank you all. Now, please, enjoy this story, and don't forget to let me know what you think.

Contact me: mdmcgriff@gmail.com.

Prologue

One of Sicily's finest hotels

People are only late to places they don't want to be. Wherever you are, you should want to be there, or why bother to go?

His name was Stone and, despite the coolness resonating from his name, he was passionate about everything he wanted to do. As he glanced at his watch, he saw again that he was not late.

The pretty front-desk clerk caught his eye as he passed under metal detectors. In the main lobby, the discreet metal detectors scanned visitors as they walked underneath them. This wasn't common knowledge, but he was ready for it. Smiling at her, he gave her a slight wink.

"Have a good day, sir," she said in Italian, her soft, sweet voice stroking his ear like silk. He returned the well wish in Italian, giving her a seductive nod, which she accepted with an even wider grin.

Passing the hotel's restaurant, he noticed tables in the stone-walled dining rooms set for the second meal of the day. Crystal wine glasses reflected the sparkle of the candlelight. He could smell the homemade breads, including the familiar scent of his favorite bread. It was made with carob flour. He could only imagine it perfected with a deliciously fresh ricotta mousse. His salivary glands went instantly into overdrive. He couldn't wait to take care of Tripoli so he could get back down here for lunch.

Antonio was a crooked mobster. Everyone in Italy knew that Antonio Tripoli could not be trusted. He did not follow the mantra of "honor among thieves." He played both sides of the law—badly. Why his government hadn't "taken care" of him was a mystery.

The Phoenix wasn't one to wait on the government to do anything, let alone take care of something. He'd found someone willing to pay him to do the job—right now. Moreover, Phoenix wasn't particular about which side of the law wanted the job done, as long as the bid was high enough.

The Phoenix was their leader. Stone was simply his right-hand man. Never questioning his command, Stone led a small team of elite and talented assassins to do the Phoenix's bidding. This job was set for three o'clock Euro time. It was now 2:59 P.M. According to the Phoenix, being late was unacceptable when doing something you wanted to do.

Of course, Stone wasn't sure anymore if doing this was what he wanted. Not anymore.

His name, Stone, was one he lived up to, even at the young age of nineteen. He was fearless.

And why not?

What is there to be afraid of?

Dying?

The thoughts brought a crooked grin to his handsome face as he approached the hallway. There he read the directory, seeing which one of the four elevators would take him to the private floor that housed the penthouse. He could have guessed, but stopping here made him appear touristy. Blending in was important when getting ready to assassinate someone.

In reality, the killing of Antonio Tripoli was not to take place here. They were to kill his men, and then take him back to their leader who, Stone knew, had planned to kill him without too much time wasted. A little interrogation and data gathering for those who were paying for the job, and then Antonio would be left for the Phoenix to dispose of.

Why they were to do this particular job this way, Stone didn't know, nor did he care. He just knew it was time consuming and he already was bored.

He'd brought three of his team here today. They were to be already in place by now, upstairs at the penthouse. He'd not received any distress calls or alarms via his receiver, so he could only assume things were going as planned.

Despite the ease of this mission so far, Stone had a bad vibe that had covered him since awakening this morning. Perhaps it had been the dream from the night before—the dream about the bird—the bird that rose from the ashes.

The Phoenix . . .

The elevator doors opened with a quiet shush. The music inside was subdued and barely audible. Stepping in, he hesitated before using the key that would allow him access to the private floor. Two large men moved into the elevator next, standing on each side of him. It was obvious they were strapped. Stone could smell a gun. It was one of his senses: sight, hearing, taste, touch, and metal detection.

They were clearly Tripoli's strongmen—hoods, shields. These men worked for Tripoli. Standing around six four or five, they looked like wrestlers from late-night American television.

Who are they trying to fool, pretending to need this elevator for purposes other than mayhem? Stone thought now while examining his ambushers. *Big and Dumb, that's who they are. Probably by name,* Stone mentally concluded.

The men spoke to each other in Italian, nevertheless, Stone understood what was being said. "How should we kill him?" one asked.

"Does it matter? He is a little niggah. We shall simply snap him like hard bread."

They laughed.

Not this day, Stone thought.

There was going to be violence here.

Stone yawned. He was getting tired of all this shit. All he wanted was to go home. He wished this was going to be his last assignment. He was through with all this. Right now, he wanted to be sitting out on his deck, watching his double drifting by on a plastic pool toy. He could see it in his mind's eye. He always saw himself as if on the outside looking in. Despite the found thought, he knew he had no such deck, and that pool was only an American suburbia dream he'd had. He dreamed of going to America and starting a life there, a life that nobody would ever know about.

"It's such a nice month to go to America, don'cha think?" he asked them in English, working hard to disguise his accent. He'd been working on an American accent for months. He yawned again, waiting for the men to decide how to proceed.

Using the key finally, the elevator bypassed floors eighteen and nineteen, and opened on the penthouse floor. The three of them stood in the elevator as if not sure who would come clean with the true intention of this meeting.

"You guys are really boring me. I'm ready to get the hell outta here," Stone said, again in English, after a few more moments of listening to their foreign exchange. "Oh, and I got your 'kill the nigga' . . . okay?" he said to them now in their own dialect.

Thinking their words had been covert and not understood, the larger of the two men abruptly stopped speaking, seemingly shocked at the young man's boldness. "Oh, you do?" he asked in broken English.

Stone saw himself in the man's eyes.

A kid, dressed in this fancy suit and expensive shoes. No doubt resembling a boy playing dress up in his rich daddy's clothes. No respect for authority. Vain, beautiful, and more importantly . . . dangerous.

The large men, who had apparently known his purpose and followed him into this elevator to kill him, smiled wickedly while opening their jackets, exposing weapons as if to say, "We got you covered." Stone simply nodded, smiling in return, and opened his jacket, showing the men he was unarmed.

"So, let's not," he said, answering their unasked request for a showdown, and pushing the elevator door button as if deciding to cancel his visit to the penthouse floor.

"You guys wanna dance? I can visit your boss later," Stone added, continuing in Italian.

The men laughed, as if eager to get the chance to beat up on this haughty "assassin," maybe even put a bullet in the back of his head.

Suddenly, right before the doors closed, they parted slightly and then ripped open as Malik, a member of his team, burst through, tossing Stone a larger weapon than the one he had concealed for emergencies.

Never travel alone . . .

Stone grabbed the man's arm and slammed the cold steel of the 9 mm against the larger man's head. He could feel the tension in his body increase.

The other man, the smaller of the two, rolled around the floor of the elevator, nursing two bullet wounds in each leg from Malik's silencer. Amid his pain, he stared upward at Stone's barrel of silent death pointed at the larger man's head.

Stone looked down at him. He wanted to feel pity, but he felt nothing. His heart again had shut down. It was a sensation he always felt at moments like this. *This was too easy. These guys are really just too dense,* Stone thought then, hoping he wouldn't have to kill the two of them. He hated killing ignorant animals. But then again, if he didn't kill them, he'd have to take them home. The thought caused a wicked chuckle to leave his lips.

Malik reached into the elevator, grabbing the larger man from Stone's grasp and placing him in front of him as a shield, while the other man lay there watching them, apparently waiting to see if either would twitch so he might have a chance to reach his concealed weapon. He went for it, thinking he saw that chance.

No such luck.

Doesn't he know?

The Phoenix team never flinches.

The seconds ticked.

Turning his attention on him, Stone's weapon whispered the sound of the bullet leaving the silencer. Stone leaned closer to the now dead man on the floor, as if making sure he was really dead. He lay on his back, no longer holding his leg. He was dead.

"Hello, anybody home?" he asked in Arabic. "Nope, his lights are out," Stone then said to Malik, filled with jest.

"Come on, man," Malik whispered anxiously, still holding the other man in front of him. "Quit fooling around. You are always fooling around," he fussed at Stone's untimely joking. Malik was from the serious land of South Africa and joking around was not what he liked to do while working.

He had a very serious nature even when not working, in Stone's opinion. "Yeah. Yeah. You're always so serious, Malik. You need to loosen up," Stone responded quietly. "You only live once. You need to break some rules every now and then," he added.

Mistaking the brief conversation between Malik and Stone as a break in concentration, the man Malik was holding as a shield slowly reached into the back of his jacket for his gun.

He was going to shoot one of them, either Malik or Stone. That was sure, and surely a bad move.

Stone noticed his subtle movement. He shot him without hesitation. Again he thought about dumb animals, how they attacked out of fear only to meet the hunter's bullet. Stone hated when dumb animals were killed.

Malik scowled as blood spattered on his handsome face. Stone raised an eyebrow, shrugging helplessly as he handed him a hanky from his breast pocket.

"Enough of your shenanigans," Malik growled, his frustration directed at Stone while snatching the hanky from him and wiping the blood away.

This brought an elongated chuckle from Stone as the blood only smeared along Malik's cheek.

Seconds were ticking . . .

Down the short hall, they dashed now. Time was running out, for surely those inside sensed the invasion. Any good criminal could feel in his bones the end of a run. Maybe that's what Stone had felt that morning after that prophetic dream. The thought of the dream unfolding right now, without him fully understanding the meaning of it, disturbed him.

Kicking in the door to Tripoli's suite, Stone couldn't help but notice the French beauty standing there, dressed to the nines. She wore red, his favorite color. The dress was low cut, and her tight cleavage begged his attention. She looked to be one of Tripoli's groupies. But her name was Capri—she was one of them.

Stone caught her with a flirtatious wink of his eye just before sending a bullet inches from her head and into the skull of the man who stood close behind her.

"Shit, Stone! Why do you always do that?" she exclaimed, ducking quickly. Retrieving the fallen man's weapon, she joined them as a partner in ridding Tripoli of his protectors one by one. The beauty was an expert marksman.

Tripoli backed his way to the door. Stone realized then he had not been taken care of as planned.

"He's getting away!" she screamed, pointing toward the door at the escaping Antonio Tripoli. She aimed her bullets around him, trying hard not to shoot him in the back. The object of the assignment was not to kill Anthony Tripoli this way. They were to take him back to their leader, the Phoenix.

Over his dead body was not supposed to be an option. The bullets didn't faze or stop him. He continued to run out the door.

Stone and Malik went after him.

Just as they stepped outside the door, an even larger man appeared. He was one neither of them had planned on. They had a head count of Tripoli's men, but apparently someone had been off in his math, as this man made six. They were only counting on there being five. The extra man's gun was aimed and ready.

"Damn," Stone growled as his column clicked empty.

"Where'd you come from?" Malik asked him before the explosion of weapons exchanged. He shot the man three times, forming a perfect triangle in his chest.

Malik had his back. As usual.

Within seconds, Malik tore off for the stairs, clearly still in hopes of catching Tripoli, who had disappeared through the emergency exit door leading down.

The third partner was Stix. "Come on," he yelled, stepping over the large body that lay at Stone's feet, the unexpected man Malik had shot.

Stix had been in the penthouse buying time with their female partner. Stone would question him later as to why he hadn't at least drugged Tripoli or otherwise gotten a better handle on this situation. Had he again changed the plan? Stix was becoming a problem.

Look at this mess, Stone thought.

Stone, instead of following, grabbed the dead man's weapon and stepped backward into the penthouse to assist Capri.

"She can take care of herself! Come on!" Stix screamed.

"Fuck that, Stix," Stone barked, before rushing back into the room.

"You're a fool. You shoulda listened to your partner," said the man holding the beauty from behind, while also coughing up blood. He had a gun pressed hard against the side of her head.

"Don't be so quick to call the kettle black," Stone sneered with sarcasm in his words, his gun aimed at the man.

All were dead in the room now, except this man. He was desperate and had little to lose. He knew that. Stone knew that.

"Go get Tripoli, Stone," the beauty whispered before the man hit her against the side of the head with the butt of the gun. "Please, go," she begged.

"Shut up! You little bitch," the gunman said.

Stone felt his eye twitch, as her eyes rolled in pain. She grabbed at the man's bloody arm that was clasped tightly around her shoulders, holding her close to him as a shield.

"Let go of her and I won't kill you," Stone lied.

The man laughed between gagging on the blood that was continually forming in his mouth. "Oh, so she is special to you, yes?" the man sneered before flicking the side of the beauty's face with his tongue.

"Tripoli's gone," Stix called as he slid back into the room, right into the tense action. He put on the breaks upon seeing the situation. His gun instantly fired, hitting the man right between the eyes, but not before the man fired on Stone, whose attention was taken away for just a second when Stix reentered the room.

The rules had been broken.

He had flinched.

The beauty screamed out as she broke from the grip of the dying man to run to Stone's side.

"Shit, Stone!" Malik panicked as he entered the penthouse. Stone groaned in pain. "Damn it."

"Oh, God." The beauty panicked, squatting down at Stone's side.

A devilish smile covered Stone's lips as the two of them noticed the blood soaking his shirt from the inside out in his belly area.

"Is he hurt bad?" Malik asked, also squatting down beside him, giving the beauty a quick glance.

"Stupid question, Malik," she fussed, looking around for something to apply pressure to Stone's wound. Ripping the shirt of one of the dead men, she held it against his rib cage over the bloody opening. "He's a man. He bleeds. He dies . . ."

"Stop now! You gotta get the fuck outta here," Stone growled, pushing her away, showing no self-pity or dereliction of his duty as her senior.

"*Vous allez être bien mon amour*," she whispered, but not so low that Malik and Stix didn't catch the affection in her voice.

"My love?" Stix asked, looking down over the scene playing out. He understood her French perfectly, although it was not his primary language.

With green eyes dazzling like diamonds, she pleaded, "Stix, help me. Please help me get him up. We have to get him back to the Phoenix."

Shaking his head emphatically, Stix barked. "No! Leave him!"

"You hate him. You've always hated him. You're jealous because he is chosen."

"Chosen? For what? You're a fool!" Stix snapped. "If he is truly as *chosen* as you believe, he'll cure himself."

"Help me, Malik," she begged now, ignoring Stix's comments, turning her attention to a more loyal friend.

"No, Stix is right. I am but a man and now a burden. Leave

me with the dead." Stone's voice was low, pained, and guttural. He resisted her efforts to pull him into a sitting position.

"He's right. We must. We must leave him," Malik told her now, accepting Stone's injuries. He pulled her hand from the grip she had on Stone's clothing. She reached for his ankles, struggling to lift his legs, then finally dropping them and falling back against the wall, all but out of hope.

"Do you love me?" Stone asked her, his voice just above a whisper upon seeing tears coming from her eyes. "Do you love me?" he asked again.

"Yes," she answered. Her voice was beaten and full of surrender.

"What will you do for me?"

"I will die for you." She spoke to him, and then looked at Malik and Stix, telling them both without a word that she had chosen to wait behind. She then reached to pick up an abandoned weapon, as if that alone would be enough to protect the two of them when the authorities came.

"And your death would have not been in vain," Stone promised. "But you will not die today."

"Keep her safe, my friend," Stone whispered in Malik's ear. Malik nodded in reply, as he gently allowed Stone to lie back onto the blood-soaked carpet and quickly turn away, hiding all emotion. "Take her!" he ordered Malik.

"No!" she screamed as Malik rose now, pulling her to her feet and pushing her toward the door. She was hysterical.

Suddenly, two shots were heard behind her and Malik's backs. The woman fought Malik like a wildcat as she knew what had occurred. Stix had finished Stone off.

These were not the rules. Of this she was certain. Stix was murdering him. If what she knew to be truth truly was, there would hell to pay for this act of treason. Capri's thoughts were jumbled, coming faster and faster with more and more clarity.

"Now he's chosen. He's chosen to die. Let's leave," Stix suggested, then quickly moved past them in the doorway.

She refused to turn around. She didn't want to see what Stix had done to Stone. She didn't want to face how badly this had all turned out.

The authorities would be coming soon and their failed mission did not need to be compounded by being caught.

Everyone knew that.

Still, she felt remorse. It hit her like a brick, and instantly she changed her mind, clawing at Malik's face, causing him to release her. She then ran back to where Stone lay with two extra bullets in his chest. "No, we won't leave you. No!" she insisted, sweat coming to her forehead as she alone attempted to lift the now unconscious man, his weight surely doubling hers.

Stix stepped toward Capri and, without warning, raised his gun to backhand her with it. Malik could hear the crack of what sounded like her skull. It caused him to jump slightly. She fell across Stone's legs.

Stix paused for a moment and then shook his head. "Damn you, Stone," he growled before hoisting the beautiful woman over his shoulder like a sack of grain.

With Malik leading the way, the three of them charged up the stairs that led to the roof of the hotel. There they awaited the drop of a ladder from the aircraft that hovered overhead. Tripoli was supposed to be on that ladder, but they had nothing to show for their day except disastrous results.

In the distance, a fire alarm could be heard from inside the hotel. The three of them looked at each other before ascending the ladder. They knew Stone, with all he had left, had started the fire, as this was his signature.

"Nothing remains in the ashes except the Phoenix," he would say.

Chapter 1

Gold studs down the length of her black leather pants protected her long legs from the wind while she rode. She couldn't help but enjoy the cool air as it whipped up under the helmet. Three inch–heeled leather boots made her clearly over six feet tall, and a custom-designed leather jacket hid the holster that housed her service revolver in a covert pocket she'd had made especially for this purpose. She pulled into The Spot and parked.

Stepping from her black Ducati motorcycle, Romia pulled the bright red helmet from her head, releasing her long raven tresses that bounced lightly around her shoulder blades. Turning the helmet slightly, she ran her hand over the emblem of the golden phoenix that covered the back of the headpiece and matched the one she had painted onto the side of the bike's monocoque frame. She then attached the helmet to the handlebar with a custom-made, short-locking bungee cord.

The symbolic bird—which she'd found intricately woven into a large tapestry in her mother's attic, while watching the two women her mother trusted most cleaning it out after she died—meant everything to her. One of the women seemed instinctively to know that she wanted to keep that tapestry. Cutting a small square from the larger piece of fabric, she handed it to Romia instead of shoving it deep into the bag she and the other woman were filling with her mother's belongings. Romia was only six, but even then felt deep inside that the bird meant she'd reunite with mother again someway, somehow, someday. It spoke to her when she was afraid and comforted her when she was worried, it replaced her mother's loving arms—it was the connection she had with the past, the past she wasn't clearly sure she actually had.

Around her neck she wore a chain. On the end of the chain a small pebble was attached. It was yet another strange but precious belonging of her mother's. She'd taken it from the jewelry box that sat on her mother's dresser. She'd taken it before the women cleaning out the house could take it. She remembered seeing her mother fondle it often, to the point of making it shine like a precious stone instead of a mere rock. It was one of the first things she took when the packing started. It was another thing she held dear.

So few things, so few memories, but they were all Romia had. Her life seemed recreated from dreams and glimpses instead of full memories of her mother.

Entering the bar Romia and her colleagues frequented, she noticed tonight it was nearly empty. Two other officers, Hank and Aston, were sitting at the front table.

"You're late, Romee!" Out of nowhere, her former partner, Keliegh Jack, appeared. He'd attended a wedding earlier that day, but had discarded his suit jacket and slacks for jeans and his common T-shirt. She'd missed seeing him all dressed up and inwardly regretted it. What a treat that would have been. But still, he looked good in the casual clothes he wore, but she would never tell him that.

Moving to where she was, his body language was possessive as he quickly blocked her from view of the other men who might want to take a look at her.

Romia recognized his moves. He was always less than discreet with how he felt about her. It had been she who held off what could have happened between them. *It just wouldn't be right . . . not with a partner*, she had reasoned in her mind.

They had never actually had the "what if" conversation, but she knew their body language said it all.

They'd been reassigned for a year now and sometimes Romia thought about those "could have happened" times. She wondered about them happening now, but so far nothing was growing between them beyond what was already there—so maybe she'd been wrong all this time about how he felt.

She and Keliegh Jack had been partners before he became a detective. He was now working with another female partner, Tamika Turner. Tamika, aka Tommy. Tommy, as most people called her, was of mixed racial descent. Romia had heard rumors that she only recently discovered that her father was a black man, a former judge who didn't claim her until he was forced to. The judge had been tied up in a murder trial, at the wrong end of it, but was freed. Perhaps the close shave with reality had given him a bite he could no longer ignore, as he soon after claimed Tommy as his daughter. Romia could relate to living her life without a father and was happy for Tommy's discovery, albeit under the not so great circumstances.

Each day, Romia looked in the mirror knowing the features on her face yelled loudly to racial ambiguity. She wondered who her father might be. It wasn't as if before her mother died she had time to answer any of those important questions Romia might need to know in life. It was many years later before Romia would realize that she and her mother were only about nineteen or twenty years apart. As young as she was, Romia often wondered if even her mother had known the answers to Romia's paternal questions.

Romia was fair. One could say she had an olive complexion in the summertime, but come winter, like now, she looked nearly white. Her dark hair was loosely curled and hung long and thick down her back, which she felt was typical of a person of mixed race. Romia's mother was fair skinned; a blonde with bright blue eyes. She would never forget her mother's eyes. Her own eyes were green.

There were no answers in the foster home she was raised in. Life wasn't bad in the foster home, just lacking in the information department. There was one good side, however: her foster parents had put her in martial arts to keep her busy.

Romia became a black belt by the age of ten and continued to seriously train, earning true marks as a master by the time she was in her late teens. For the others in the foster home it was just fun, but for Romia it was more than just something to do, it was life changing. Each move was perfection or she wouldn't stop practicing until it was. She fought hard and with a desperation that gave the impression that her life depended on it. By the age of twenty-five she was a fifth-level black belt, and had since climbed the ranks with determination. She was now twenty-eight years old and approaching the ninth level in the standard karate training. Yet her sensei had taught her many secret moves. He'd taught her moves he'd brought with him from his homeland.

Romia's fighting skills were amazing and beyond the comprehension of many. It was as if she was born to fight, like it was in her blood. He didn't need to teach her much. In reality, she had surpassed the levels of her training, but just could not be awarded any higher due to the rules of competition.

As she followed Keliegh over to the bar, she noticed Keliegh's date was sitting there in a hideous pink taffeta dress, but, with a body like hers, who cared, right? Keliegh always dated Barbie-doll blondes. You'd think a brother would have more imagination. But he didn't. He liked fake women who didn't give him a lot of lip. Maybe that was why the two of them hadn't gotten anywhere. Fake, Romia was not, and as far as lip, she was always putting him in his place with a little neck jecking and what he called his mama's attitude: no ifs ands, or buts. She didn't say much, but when she did, every-one knew she was serious.

Barefoot and tired, the little girlie he was with looked like she needed a drink. *A dress like that could drive one to drink,* Romia inwardly dogged while sliding up on the stool next to the girl, who had her feet up on the empty stool next to her. Maybe Keliegh had been rubbing her feet. Who knew? Maybe Romia was a little bit jealous. *Whatever.* "I see you're digging that dress," she remarked to Shashoni, Keliegh's date, while grinning wickedly.

Shashoni rolled her eyes. "We just left the reception hall. I haven't had time to get home and all that, unlike Keliegh who changed in the car. God! I needed a damn drink. Quick," she answered, apparently still waiting for her drink that was clearly long overdue since having been ordered.

"You had a drink at the reception. Quite a few," Keliegh said, trying to speak in a lower than usual voice. Shashoni was pretty close to drunk, Romia could tell now that she'd actually looked closer. She also noticed Keliegh's overprotective tone.

Finally, the waiter brought her drink. It was a stiff one. Reaching for it, Keliegh intercepted it, pushing it out of her reach. "What do you think you're doing?" she asked, reaching for the drink again.

He blocked her hand. "Enough, Shoni, you've had enough."

Shashoni looked around, to see if anyone was watching their exchange. Romia too felt uncomfortable. Perhaps it was because the spotlight was suddenly on them, or so it felt.

"Here's your drink, Romee," the bartender said to her, drawing her attention back suddenly to her own business.

Standing and turning to the bar to gather her club soda, a man reaching for his drink a little too closely bumped her. Her arms rose over her head out of reflex and to keep from spilling her water on everyone. "Hey, watch it," she yelped when he suddenly copped a quick feel of one of her breasts in the process. She pushed him away from her with a shove that normally would send someone to the ground, spilling the drink anyway.

"Watch it, ya asshole," Keliegh quickly added, giving him another shove for good measure. Still, he merely stumbled and bumbled his way out the door.

Romia's first instinct was to go after the guy who bumped her, but before heading out, she noticed a strange odor on her jacket. "What is this?" Romia asked, sniffing her sleeve. She'd never tasted liquor, having made the vow to never drink spirits since a drunk driver had killed her mother.

They were walking together when the car had come barreling around the corner right at her. Romia would never forget it. Her mother pushed Romia out of the way right before the car struck, and instead of killing Romia, the car hit her mother. The impact of the hit threw her over the hood of the car like a big hand slapping at a small bug. It sent her crashing through the windshield. Her beautiful dress was shredded. The blood sprayed everywhere. Her blue eyes, open and piercing. The screaming. Her screams . . .

"I said I was sorry for what I said," Shashoni confessed, sounding less than sober, rambling on, apparently not noticing Keliegh's distraction with Romia's spilled drink.

"Smells like booze," Keliegh answered after he too sniffed her leather.

"What is this, Mike?" Romia asked the bartender.

"Sorry, musta given you that loser's drink." Mike shrugged absently. "I've never done that before."

"I'm over that, Shoni." Keliegh shrugged, turning his attention back to Shashoni, who had laid her head on her folded arms. "I'm worried about your drinking right now."

"Look at my jacket! You messed up my jacket with this stuff. I don't drink this mess, Mike!" Romia fussed, feeling inexplicably enraged. She had been having a hard time controlling her temper lately. She was feeling hormonal, or tired, or something off, but lately she got angry very easily. The breathing exercises she used while meditating were barely capturing her inner emotions, barely keeping her grounded.

"I said I was sorry," Mike pleaded, though sounding unconvincing in his attempt to prove that he felt he'd done anything wrong. Romia was fuming. Keliegh turned his attention back to her.

"Calm down, Romee. It's just a little spill. I care about you," he said, turning his head back quickly to Shashoni. His head resembled a person watching tennis.

"Since when?" growled Shashoni, grabbing the drink and tossing it back before he could stop her. He shook his head.

"I didn't know you felt . . ." Keliegh began before Shashoni lowered the near-empty glass slowly from her full lips. She glared at him, as if daring him to expose the content of their private matters.

"You knew I did." She turned the tumbler up, draining the very last drop.

Romia understood immediately what was going on here. Shoshoni had fallen for Keliegh and made the mistake of telling him. That was obvious even without them finishing their sentences. Romia could see love in Shashoni's eyes, and maybe a little in Keliegh's too. And besides, she'd seen this scene play out one too many times. Shashoni must have said the L word or even, heaven forbid, the M word, and now it was all ruined. Keliegh wasn't husband material. Romia could have told her that. But then again . . .

Who cares? Right now, her jacket had booze on it. In her mind, her problem was a lot bigger than Keliegh hitting and quitting some chick in an ugly pink dress.

"I need a towel. Dang! You gotta towel back there?" Romia asked, leaning over the counter.

Still in the throes of his heated conversation with Shasho-ni, Keliegh whispered, "We were partners." Clearly, he was hoping to keep his words private, but Romia heard.

Why does he have to explain that to this bimbo? Romia instantly thought, but did not ask. "She's like my sister. I can't see her any other way. Why are you buggin'?"

Shashoni smirked and pulled her foot free from Keliegh's hand. He had taken it as if he was going to start rubbing or re-rubbing it after lecturing her on the protocol of being with him and where she fit in. Partner first, former partner second, and then, maybe, you! Romia understood that! This chick was crazy if she thought she would ever be placed before her—or Tamika Turner. Shashoni then stood and smoothed the frou-frou pink dress down. Sliding her feet into painful-looking pumps, she stomped from the bar, leaving Keliegh with the tab.

While he dug for the money to pay, Romia noticed the slightly staggering young Shashoni heading out the door into the night, in this not so nice neighborhood that clearly she didn't belong in. Romia rushed to follow her, not waiting for the towel.

"Shashoni!" she called as the door shut in her face. Romia was thinking how crazy Shashoni looked taking off in that pink dress. "Let me take you home. I mean, sure you have on that lovely dress but . . ." she began, pushing open the door and heading outside. Looking around for Shashoni, she couldn't see her, only the dust of an apparent patron's car that was leaving the parking lot. Suddenly, the night sounds were added to by the sounds of a scuffle, which had increa-sed recognizably in the darkness near where her motorcycle was parked. It was indeed a struggle, a fight, an altercation. "Shashoni?" Romia went immediately on alert.

Chapter 2

Reaching the back of the bar, heading toward her bike, a tall, agile man swung on her as soon as she cleared the corner. Her reflexes were catlike and she pulled back, his blow missing by mere inches. Sensing his every move, and he hers, made it feel like she was fighting her shadow . . . or a sensei. He mimicked her technique, blow for blow, as if having studied her moves. Had they fought before, maybe in competition? Did she know him? He wore black, resembling the attire of a ninja, and in the night, all she could see were his eyes, which glowed against the light that hung off the roof of the tavern.

Attempting to look in his eyes, Romia kicked and punched quickly, hoping not to lose eye contact with the stranger for more than a millisecond. He blocked each blow with precision.

Just then, a woman screamed. "Shashoni!" Romia called out, thinking it was Keliegh's date being attacked somewhere in the distance. The woman screamed again. "She killed him!"

The attacker struck. Distracted by the woman's scream, Romia caught a blow that drew blood from her lip. When she stumbled back from the hard blow, the attacker took advantage of the time to scurry away. Romia's first instincts were to go after him, but the woman's bellows drew her attention in that direction. She felt her mouth. The blood had started flowing from the small break in the taut skin of her full bottom lip.

Reaching the strange white woman she'd never seen before,

she saw the body of a man lying face down. The woman stood there screaming while all the color drained from her face. "Can you shut up?" Romia demanded, looking around for Shashoni.

Romia squatted next to the body, but before she could do her job, the bar began to empty with spectators headed in her direction.

"She killed him," the woman screeched, pointing at Romia in a tattling fashion.

The men and women began to scramble, heading for cars to avoid the questions from the cops who were sure to come. Others ran back into the bar to get Hank and Aston and Keliegh, no doubt, because within seconds they came out.

"What are you talking about?" Romia asked, realizing only now that the woman was accusing her.

"Freeze, Romee!" Hank yelled, drawing his gun on her.

"Hank, you're kidding, right?" Romia asked, slowly attempting to rise from the body of the man, which now had blood trickling slowly out from under him.

The blood from her face was on her hands, and she could easily see how bad this all looked, yet she had not touched the dead man, not even to check a pulse.

"Stay where you are and put your hands up!" Aston Mitchell, another officer from her precinct, demanded.

"Move away, lady!" Aston yelled at the woman, who then quickly ran toward the bar. Romia wished she had gotten a better look at her, because she had a strange feeling this was to be the last she would see of the woman outside of a courtroom.

"Romee, what the hell happened?" Keliegh asked as he quickly pushed through the growing crowd.

Glancing up at him, her green eyes were aglow against the light of the full moon. Her mouth was now covered with blood from the wound that at first had seemed so minor. She bled easily from her full lips and, therefore, usually made a point of not getting hit in the mouth.

"He went that way." Reaching under her jacket, she realized then her gun was gone. Her eyes immediately focused on the one laying next to the body. It was hers. "What the . . ." She picked it up.

"Drop it, Romee!" Hank yelled.

"What the hell are you doing, Hank? It's Romee!" Keliegh jumped between the officers and Romia, who was staring at the gun: the weapon that had apparently killed the man laying face down in the dirt. It was the man from the bar who had touched her breast. This didn't look good at all.

Keliegh was looking stunned, and a bit confused, but stood his ground. There was no way he was going to arrest her, or allow Hank or Aston to either.

"I . . . I didn't . . ." Romia stammered, hearing sirens in the distance. *Someone must have called*, she thought.

"Drop the gun," Keliegh whispered over his shoulder while standing between the drawn weapons and Romia.

"Get out of the way, Kel," Hank ordered.

"No, now come on . . . This is crazy! Get that woman out here to tell what she saw," Keliegh insisted.

"I don't know what happened, Aston. I don't know what's going on. It happened too fast," Romia said to Aston, who looked determined to arrest her.

"Romia Smith, you're under arrest. You have the right . . ." Aston began, while pulling out his handcuffs from the back of his trousers. He stepped forward, but Keliegh refused to allow him to get close enough to put the cuffs on.

"Get out of the way!" Aston ordered, stepping toward Keliegh as if to go through him. Aston was going to prove he had no hesitation arresting a colleague.

Suddenly, Romia dropped the gun, pushed Keliegh aside, and stepped forward, snatching Aston's weapon from him and dismantling it with one hand before twisting his arm behind him. She had to get away before the squad car arrived.

Keliegh swung on Hank before he could fire.

Aston freed himself from Romia's loose grip. She'd not really tried to restrain him so much as buy a moment to think. He swung on her, but Romia easily ducked back and flat-hand punched him across the face, stunning him.

Everyone knew of her fighting skills, but also her restrictions. She could kill him within seconds—Aston knew it as well as she did. She was not allowed to street fight. It was all but illegal for her, but there was no way she was going to jail tonight. "Come on, Romee," Aston said, holding his cheek while moving lightly on his feet, as if contemplating taking on the challenge of fighting her. He charged at her only to have her hit him twice, this time with a closed fist. She held back on the power of her punch, but still drew blood from his nose. He cursed her and swung again, but she easily ducked the telegraphed punch.

Hearing the sirens closing in, she knew time was running out on this game. Aston kicked at her; he'd apparently been practicing his karate moves, but was no competition. She caught the kick, turning his foot just enough to cause pain but not break. He yelped and crumbled to the ground. Standing in a guarded stance, she began inching her way clear to break for her bike.

Keliegh had wrestled the gun from Hank and tossed it aside. They were both breathing heavily from their momentary tussle before Hank pulled a smaller weapon from the back of his pants.

"Don't try it, Romia. I'll shoot you," Hank said.

Romia raised her hands. "Stop! This has to stop!"

Again Keliegh jumped between Hank and Romia, tackling Hank to the ground. Hank's gun went off, but the shot ricocheted in the darkness, missing Romia by a mile as she leapt onto the seat of her bike. It started up without delay, almost as if sensing her need for speed. She took off without even putting on her helmet, which was still held tight to the bike by its cord.

The squad car pulled in just as she swerved around it, spitting up dust as she avoided the head-on collision. The officer behind the wheel hung a tight U-turn and pursued her. She could see the car right on her tail in her rearview mirror.

Why are they not listening to me? Why is this happening? Who was that woman? Something didn't feel right. Something wasn't right. But Romia wasn't going to stop and ask questions. Pushing the bike to top speed, causing the front wheel to rise a couple of feet off the ground before gripping the road, she grew the distance between them. She had to get out of there, but where would she go?

Still hearing the sirens close behind her, she turned the bike into the first alleyway she approached. She was in an area known as the Palemos; it was a ghetto and basically abandoned by the city dollars. There were many dark and deserted hiding places, and she planned to take advantage of one of them. They would be calling for backup, if they hadn't already, so she knew she needed to get off the main streets to get around easier, faster, and without much detection. They would never find her in this neighborhood—everyone on a beat knew that if a suspect ducked into the Palemos you could forget finding him unless you had a good snitch. Romia was certain the cops would never find her once she got on foot.

Screeching the bike to a halt, she quickly dismounted, leaving the helmet hooked on the bungee. The golden phoenix glowed against the moonlight. Her heart was tearing apart as she freed herself of the custom jacket that everyone recognized and knew she wore—and that she loved—tossing it aside. Looking back as she started to run off, the regret was too much; dashing back, she ripped the helmet from the bungee and slammed it on her head before looking around and then upward for a fire escape. Finding one, and without pulling the ladder down, she jumped high, gripping the bar tightly while pulling herself up to the first rung and flipping her legs over her head and through the bars. Acrobatically, she then pulled herself toward her feet, flipping over the railing and climbing five stories until she found a broken window with an opening big enough to climb through. She ducked inside the empty office building.

Chapter 3

Memories

"Mommy, why my hair is brown and yours is yellow?" the small child, Romia, asked her mother. She had lightly tugged at the ends of it that hung long down her back.

Her mother responded, smiling down at her while picking the healthier box of cereal off the top rack of the shelf. "My hair is yellow because the sun made it that way."

"Will the sun do that to my hair one day?"

Bending down, she kissed her on the cheek. "The sun will never need to. You are safe as you are. You are blessed and safe as you," she added. "But if you ever feel as though you are not safe, you will simply ask the sun to make your hair yellow, and your eyes blue"—she bent down close to Romia's ear—"when they are actually green."

Romia thought about those words all day. She was a deep-thinking child who was affected by every word from her mother's lips. Each word touched her deeply and lessons taught would never be forgotten—stored deeply, true—but never forgotten. Her mother laughed after speaking to her in the riddle-like fashion. She often spoke that way to her. Thinking back on her, Romia sometimes wondered if perhaps English wasn't her first language, although she would be hard-pressed to figure out what other language her mother could have spoken, considering English was the only language she heard from her.

"Let's see if Mrs. Thurston is ready to leave the store," she said, moving her basket toward another aisle. They often shopped with the older woman who lived next door. Romia had come to view that woman as a grandmother. When her mother died, she wasn't surprised to find her being one of the women helping to pack up her mother's things. She was surprised to find that she wasn't going to be living with her, but thinking back now, surely the woman was too old to care for a child her age. Even then she had to be around fifty.

Suddenly, her mother stopped as if frozen in time. She stared off into space and then spun on her heels, causing Romia to look in the same direction. At the end of the aisle stood a tall, dark, mysterious-looking man who was not even looking their way, yet her mother became instantly fearful. Romia could sense her feelings through her hand that tightly grasped her own.

"Sweetheart," she said calmly in Romia's ear after lifting her onto her hip, "we'll wait in the car for Mrs. Thurston, okay?"

Romia looked at the groceries. "But what about—"

"Never mind that," she answered, moving her quickly through the next aisle and out of the store. She continually looked back toward the door of the store until they reached the car.

"You were taking awhile. I got finished and came out to the car," Mrs. Thurston said, smiling all the while.

"Wonderful," her mother snapped quickly, unlocking the door for Mrs. Thurston to get in.

"Where is your fo—" Mrs. Thurston began to ask before Romia's mother all but shoved her into the car.

She opened the back door and hoisted Romia inside. "Put on your seatbelt, sweetheart," she said, sounding nearly out of breath, still glancing back at the store.

Romia obeyed.

They rushed home. Romia remembered her mother pacing

most of the evening, yet breaking into a bright smile every time their eyes met. "I love you with more than all my heart," she said.

This was but one strange memory Romia had of her mother. Some would come and go quickly, oddly. But this one would play over and over, the same way each time.

Chapter 4

Almost instantly, the light beams shone around the room and Romia could hear voices floating up from down below. "If she's on foot we'll never find her," someone said. The sounds of sirens poured into the alley; there were at least four squad cars.

"I know, have you ever clocked her? She's fast. I trained with her once and she was amazing. She—"

"Quit talking about her like she's a superwoman," another office said.

"I'm just sayin' . . . we're not going to find her."

Romia moved close in to the wall as the light flew across the room. "This is crazy," someone admitted. "Did she really kill somebody?"

"Anybody see anything?"

"Who was the victim?"

"I hear it was another cop." The voices continued until finally the sounds grew muffled and distant.

"Romia killed a cop?" The voices sounded like a crowd growing as the officers below scoured the alleyway. Without the ladder being lowered, they would be hard-pressed to assume she was in one of the buildings. Even if they reasoned on it, it would take a psychic to figure out she was in this particular building—unless she made a sound, which she couldn't do now if she tried.

Finally, and suddenly, they were gone.

Stiff with mortification and shock, Romia didn't move for

what felt like hours. Standing in the darkness still wearing her helmet, she felt sick, nausea forming deep in the pit of her belly until finally, as if awakening from a half sleep, she slowly removed the helmet and set it quietly on the floor—afraid to make a peep. *I'll be okay here for the night, I guess,* she thought, her eyes adjusting to the dark room lightened only by the reflection off the liquor store across street. Its neon sign showed bright down the alleyway as the night began to come alive. It was always that way in the Palemos at night.

Normally, Romia would walk the streets unbothered by the elements. She was fearless—especially when working a beat. She was a plainclothes cop, although most people knew her, so working undercover was generally a waste of time. Besides, a reputation like hers traveled fast. She was tough, but trustworthy. She had a lot of friends on the street. Tonight, she was counting on that, because tomorrow she needed to get some answers and get them quick before her brothers in the law came after her again.

Romia thought about Keliegh and what he must have gone through having interfered the way he had, allowing her to escape arrest. She needed to get a hold of him, but surely he was either detained or being watched. *Maybe Tamika.* Exhausted, Romia couldn't even finish the thought. She sat on the dirty floor, burying her face in her hands. Closing her eyes, mentally spent, she leaned her head back against the wall until soon she dozed off, jerking fitfully every few moments.

Suddenly, she jerked fully awake. The presence of the shadowy figure brought her to full alert . . . That, plus the gun pressing against her forehead. "I can't believe you're asleep," the shadow said, chuckling wickedly with a hint of disappointment in his tone. "I've been holding this here for at least a minute. I could have killed you ten times."

"Once would be plenty," Romia answered, bringing her leg up between the shadows legs with lightening speed, but he was faster, blocking her. She slapped the gun away only to catch a blow to the head from the opposite hand. Unfazed, she knew the hit had been pulled back. It was as if the shadow was sparring with her and had no plans to kill her. With the agility and speed of a puma, she jumped to a crouching position, blocking quick-coming blows until she maneuvered herself out of the corner she was in. "What do you want? Who are you?"

"As if I would answer you. What is the honor in that? The challenge?" the shadow spoke. His words came without any show of strain or effort while he swung on her effortlessly, maintaining remarkable speed.

Finally, he stepped back from her and stood in the darkness. Dressed completely in black and with his face covered except for his eyes, his features were indistinguishable. But she knew the shadow as male; it was obvious by his build and heavy masculine voice—although he had masked it, whispering huskily when he spoke. As if both sensing the same feelings, she reached for her helmet, but not before he grabbed it. "Aw, the phoenix," he said, smacking his lips sarcastically. "Elusive little bird . . . Rises from the ashes, they say. Tsk tsk. As if only you deserved to wear it."

Romia said nothing. She was thinking too hard, trying to get ahead of this shadow, trying to figure out what was happening to her. "I do deserve it," she finally blurted, sounding like a little girl instead of the tough cookie everyone knew her to be.

"I'll determine that, but as for now, you're just a criminal—a murderer."

"I didn't kill that man."

The shadow laughed. "I know that. You were playing with me behind the bar when it happened. But then again, I'm a terrible alibi, don't you think?"

He was right, he was no better than the mysterious one-armed man from the movies. No one would believe her if she told them of the encounter with the shadow. She'd have to prove her innocence by finding the killer. It was the only way.

"Who killed him?"

"Who do you think?"

"I don't know. I . . ." Romia thought about the scene. "The woman!" Romia gasped. The man chuckled. "Who was she? You know, don't you?"

"Too easy, but a good start." The shadow started for the window, but Romia charged at him to get her helmet back. A back kick sent her tumbling. This time he did not hold back. The blow stunned her and she hesitated before getting up, assessing her ribs. "You'll get this back when you deserve it," he said, disappearing out the window, taking her helmet with him.

Romia struggled to her feet and ran to the window, only to see an empty alley below. *How did he know I was here?* she asked herself, feeling the chill of violation. Again she looked around the room. She needed to sleep. It was late, but she knew time was of the essence. Tomorrow would be too late. The trail would be cold. She had to get some answers . . . now!

She had to get out of her boots and get into some travel gear. She had no gun, no jacket, no vehicle, and now . . . no lucky charm. All this dawned on her as she slinked through the dark streets, darting in and out of alleyways, avoiding streets where the night people were foraging for food and finding places to sleep warmly.

Surviving.

She felt vulnerable without her bike, jacket, and helmet. Those belongings that bore the symbol that represented her strength were missing now. The police had taken her bike; it was gone when she came down from the building to see if, just in case, they had left it. No such luck. Looking around, she assumed they had her jacket, too.

Framed and hanging on the wall in her apartment, the tapestry was all she had left and she was determined to get it before the police got to her place. Like a cat in the night she moved through the crowded streets undetected without her normal attire.

Chapter 5

In the meantime somewhere over the Atlantic.

The largest of the three men spoke little English. His native tongue was Arabic. He was Egyptian. The other two were from Cairo and their English was clearly understood. The airport lines were less complicated for English-speaking foreigners.

They each carried bags that gave them the appearance of traveling businessmen who also wanted to enjoy a little California fun. Floral shirts and sunscreen also set the stage for their American vacation.

Settling into the seats, they smiled at the flight attendant. She was tall and blond.

"You gentlemen want champagne?" she asked, making her way through first class.

"Yes, I believe we do," one of the men answered for all three. The woman smiled. It was obvious her eyes caught sight of the ring on the Egyptian's finger. The large ring clustered with diamonds in an odd shape on his middle finger had to have dazzled her.

"Your ring is lovely. Fraternity?" she asked. Another of the English-speaking men looked at the ring and then smiled at her, lifting the Egyptian's hand so she could get a closer look.

"It's a phoenix. Do you know what that is?"

Her face scrunched up a little in a cute way. "Um, a mythological bird that, um, rises from the ashes, right?"

"You're close. It is a beautiful woman born to rule. She's elusive and seductive and unaware of her power. With just a glance, she can set a world on fire and walk away unburned," the man answered her. "Yet, she's far from mythical. She's standing right in front of everyone," he added. The flight attendant smiled and blushed as if having just received a compliment. She had no idea what the man was talking about.

Chapter 6

"So you were there? Tell me what happened," the officer from internal affairs barked. He'd been questioning Keliegh for the past hour about what he'd seen and not seen, and then, as if Keliegh hadn't heard the questions, he asked them again—backward. It was bad enough that it was late and he was tired and not thinking clearly, but then they had further confused him by taking him to an interrogation center outside of his precinct.

"I told you everything. By the time I got outside, Romia was kneeling over some dead guy, or whatever, and it was all circumstantial. The woman was screaming that Romia had shot the guy. But, no, I didn't see her shoot anybody."

"But you say she was all bloody."

"No, I didn't say she was all bloody. I said her lip was busted, she bleeds easily from the mouth, and—"

"How do you know that?"

Keliegh grimaced at the question. "We were partners. You learn stuff like that about your partner."

"Did she fight a lot? Get smacked in the chops a lot? What?"

"She never fought in the street. But like in competition, if she took a hit to the face, she bled . . . a lot. It would usually take her out of a match."

"I heard she knew the guy she killed."

That was it. Keliegh stood. "Can I go now? I mean, you've accused her of murder enough for one night. Don't you think you should be out there looking for the person who shot that guy?"

"Who else coulda done it?"

"The woman maybe? Who was she? Nobody seems to know!"

"What woman?" the Internal Affairs officer asked.

Just then, two more IA agents burst into the interrogation room. Keliegh didn't know them, either. Strangely enough, Keliegh had never met any of the men he'd seen here tonight. He didn't know these cats from Adam. He was ready to bust one of them in the mouth and get the hell outta there. He'd never been at the office of internal affairs before and he had to admit, they were serving him up every dish from the intimidation café—but he wasn't shaken. Keliegh wanted nothing more than to get out of there so he could find Romia. She was scared. He'd seen it in her eyes. It was a look he'd never seen before and so it had to be fear . . . *what else?* Surely it wasn't malice. *She didn't kill that guy . . . there was no way. For what? Feeling her up and causing her to get alcohol spilled on her jacket?* Shooting him would have been rather extreme—even for her. Keliegh wasn't buying it as easily as Aston and Hank were. He'd seen them come from another room while he waited to be called. They avoided eye contact with him, which let him know they'd sold her out. *Pricks.*

"We're gonna be watching you, Detective Jack. You have a problem with the directional signal on your loyalty gauge. She killed a cop tonight."

"What?" Keliegh exploded, standing straight up. The men who came into the room stood as if guarding the door. Keliegh had to wonder if this clown was about to take him on a few rounds. Unconsciously, he puffed up just a little, flexing and breathing a little harder.

"Now calm your ass down. What I'm saying is, you are all ready to hang up your badge for your ex-partner, who is clearly as guilty as sin, and—"

"And you're crazy." Keliegh fanned his hand toward Maxwell as if to say, "Bah humbug." "I don't know what Hank and that punk Aston told you but, excuse me, Romia is a loyal cop. A good cop."

"A cop who snapped tonight and killed a fellow officer because he touched her."

"Oh, my ga . . ." Keliegh swagged his head in a negative argument. "That is so off base. You are so off base. What, did Aston and Hank tell you that too?"

Maxwell Huntington just looked at Keliegh with an expression that read,

"You can go, Detective Jack," Maxwell Huntington, the head of IA, barked, dismissing Keliegh without further discussion. "You're suspended until further notice."

Keliegh stood his ground for a moment before shaking his head in disgust at this whole matter and walking out. He wasn't sure what to feel but he knew he had to find Romia.

Chapter 7

The block was quiet, but that was somewhat normal for Romia's neighborhood. She lived on the "good" end of the Palemos, if you wanted to call it that. But then again, Romia had little fear, so Keliegh never really worried about where she lived as much as he worried about her, as a whole. Like now, he was worried sick. His stomach was even starting to cramp up. Fighting the growing emotions, blaming it on the late-night street activities, thoughts about his career and the strong feeling he was being tailed, Keliegh didn't give into the fact that his only focus was on Romia's safety. Keliegh didn't give into the fact that his concern over her was clouding his reason. Why would she have come home?

Idiot! Keliegh thought, mentally bashing himself. He just realized then, too, that he'd not even given Shashoni a second thought as he whipped into Romia's complex.

Locking the door of his car, he looked around for stalkers. It wasn't as if he was hard to spot. Standing an easy six three or four in flat bare feet, if he was on the run he'd be caught in a moment. Maybe that was what was bothering him about Romia. She was not the kind of person who blended in well either. Maybe that was what he found so fascinating about her. She was so . . . different.

Keliegh reached her door and slid his spare key in the lock. He'd had a spare since they were partners. She reluctantly gave him one after having accepted his—for emergencies, of course. One day, not long after he was promoted to detective, he found his spare on his desk; she'd returned it. He wasn't about to do the same and return the key to her place. He had his pride, and . . .

". . . And good thing, too," he mumbled, turning the lock and easing the door open. Not sure if his prints were still on anything in her place, considering how long it'd been since he'd visited, he made note of all he touched: the light, the door, the chair. The chair was thrown over. "Daaaamn!" he exclaimed, noticing that more than the chair was out of place. The apartment was a mess. He could see this as soon as his eyes focused to the dim light.

The living room had been professionally, albeit ruthlessly, tossed. *Looking for what? Who knows!* Keliegh stepped lightly as he moved through the apartment, noting all the damage. "Cops? Why would they trash her place? This wasn't cops. Who did this?" he asked himself, closing her refrigerator door that lay open. Romia's bedroom was in no better condition than the living room: toiletries all over the floor, mirror on the medicine cabinet busted as if by a fist. He noticed her papers scattered all about her bed. He noticed her pictures torn off her walls; all the frames were broken. It was hard to tell if anything had been actually stolen with all the damage. *Her stereo is still here, her television set . . .*

Her answering machine was blinking. Looking around, knowing he could be tampering with possible evidence that may be be important, Keliegh pushed the play button. The caller spoke in a foreign language that Keliegh did not initially pick up.

"Wrong number, I guess," he reasoned, continuing to look around the room. He noticed a picture Romia had of the two of them in uniform. They'd been friends a long time. He picked it up and closely examined it before tucking it in his shirt pocket. He then saw a picture of a woman holding a baby. He looked at the woman. She had Romia's rarely shared smile. "Is this your mom?" he asked aloud. Sighing heavily, he tucked that picture in his pocket as well. "Where are you, Rome? Who did this?" he asked himself again before leaving.

Chapter 8

What a day it had been. It seemed as though whatever could go wrong went wrong. She had tried with all her might to make it to the wedding, or maybe she didn't try all that hard. Seeing Shashoni in pink taffeta wasn't what she felt the need to break her neck to do.

But surely that scene would have been better than this one. Files lost, cap'n all crazy, and cramps like you wouldn't believe. Tommy wanted to laugh, cry, and maybe kick somebody's ass all at the same time. But instead she cleaned up reports. She was crazy about Keliegh but the boy couldn't write a report if it meant his life.

"You hitting The spot?" Aston and Hank had asked her on their way out hours ago. Her eyes must have said it all as they held up their hands in surrender. He heard Aston call her a bitch but she didn't even care enough to call him on it. At that moment in time, she was, and she knew it. It was around one now, nearly time for those who had gone home earlier to be on their way back in. She glanced at her watch.

"I'ma go home and soak in a hot—"

"Turner! I need to talk to you for a minute," the captain had called to her.

"Shit," she grumbled. It was a whistle and she caught it. "Alls I know is they better not run," she grumbled, heading into his office to get the assignment.

"Got a big one. It's a shooting out in the view. Looks domestic," he said, handing her the address. "Take Bishop with you."

"Bishop? Why don't I just call Jack? He's due in about an hour . . ."

"Take Bishop," the captain barked.

Tommy felt her eyes roll but tried to fight it. She couldn't stand Canasta Bishop. Maybe it was because Keliegh had slept with her. "Come on," was all Tommy said to her, slapping her hand on Canasta's desk. Canasta looked up at her with surprise showing.

"Me?"

"You."

They walked out the front of the station just as Hank was making his way back in. "Wow!" was all he said.

"Wow what?" Tommy responded, half bored, half interested.

"Man, is Jack in deep."

"What?" Canasta asked. Tommy consciously glared at her.

"Romia shot somebody tonight and then kicked Aston's ass and then pulled a gun on me and Jack. Tried to kill us—"

"Romia?" both Tommy and Canasta said at the same time.

"Yeah, it was crazy. She was all wild-eyed. I think she's doing crack or something for sure. She just snapped," he said, holding out his hands and bending them quickly as if breaking an invisible stick.

"Where is Keliegh now?"

"Well, he got all in the way of the arrest. I mean, he let her get away, so you know his ass is on the chopping block. Last I saw him he was under the light with IA."

"Oh my God! Canasta, go tell Cap'n you and Hank took this whistle—"

"But—"

"Just go tell him . . . Shit. I'll take the heat. He can fire me or whatever tomorrow, but I gotta go," Tommy said, leaping off the steps of the precinct and jogging to her car. She was done for the night and no further plans for Calgon to take her away.

Chapter 9

Reaching his house, he noticed the unmarked car across the street. "Wow, that's discretion. I'm sure she'll walk right into this trap." Keliegh chuckled sarcastically, loosening his door key from among the mess of keys on his ring. Keliegh thought about Tamika "Tommy" Turner, his current partner. She'd not called all evening, which was a surprise. Normally she was the first to hear a whistle in the station house—especially with his having been suspended. Surely she was shocked to get the news. Surely his suspension was all over the place by now. *Those IA guys were tough.*

And where the hell is Shashoni? He'd not heard a peep from her either, now that he thought about her.

He glanced at his watch. He needed to call his uncle. It was late, but his uncle was probably still on duty.

Keliegh's uncle, Lawrence Miller, was a homicide detective in the Palemos district. Surely he'd gotten wind of this case and was probably on it, or pretty close to it at least. The body fell pretty close to his beat. Keliegh could get some untainted information from him. If nothing else, he could get some advice on what to do about his former partner being accused of a murder that there was no way she could commit, and even more advice on what to do if she did. The number rang as he jingled his keys at the door.

"Miller."

"Hey, Unk."

"Yeah."

"What's the news?"

"Same ol'."

"So you didn't hear?"

"I hear well."

"Shooting at The Spot. Did it fall on you?"

"Hey!" he called out. "Anybody catch a whistle at The Spot?"

Keliegh waited for his uncle to get an answer.

"Nah, nobody here got nothing. Why?"

"My partner—well, former partner, you know, I told you about her—Romia." Keliegh opened his door of his apartment and stood in the threshold, but didn't reach in to turn on the light. "Um, there was a little trouble . . . a little misunderstanding."

"Spit it out."

"She might be in some trouble. There was a shooting about three hours ago and, well, she didn't wait for questions. Guy was supposed to be a cop."

"What the hell! She killed a fellow officer?"

"Look, don't get all crazy! She didn't do it. I know she didn't. I had never seen that guy before in my life. IA said he was a cop, though. I mean, who knows, right? Nobody knew the guy, right?"

"You don't know anything. And if she's on the run for shooting a brother then she's trouble. If we get this call and we find her, we ain't gonna play nice with her. If she's a sw—"

"She's not! God, I hate that word. She's not crazy. It was an accident or something. I was there, but damned if I know what happened. One minute we were having a drink, the next she's outside over a body and Hank and Aston got guns on her. She freaked—I would have too. I thought you guys were on it because somebody's already been at her place. Did a bang up job."

"We wouldn'a got a search warrant that quick. Hell, three

hours, we'd still be at the scene. You saying IA is already on it?"

"Yeah, already hauled my ass in. You know anybody named Maxwell something?"

"Maxwell something? Can you be a bit more vague for me here?"

"Hell, maybe he was CIA, who knows?" Keliegh was digging for answers, hoping one would just fall into his lap by accident. Nothing. His uncle wasn't being helpful at all.

Stepping all the way into the dark foyer of his small duplex apartment, he pondered his next words. Just then, he thought he heard something coming from inside his apartment. Glancing at the officer in the car across the street sitting mindlessly, staring into space, he wondered if he had another stakeout cop in his apartment. "I have to call you back," he said to his uncle, hanging up quickly. He closed the door and drew his weapon. "I'm armed, I'm a cop, and I'm gonna blow your head off if you think you're in here robbing me. If you're a cop and you're here to babysit me, I'll kick your ass," he called, pointing the gun upward while sliding along the walls deeper into the dark apartment, until he was standing in the living room.

"Keliegh," Romia whispered.

"Romee, how the hell did you get in here, they have my place surrounded—sort of," Keliegh whispered back, startled to hear her voice. He was not sure where she was in the apartment until his gun left his hands from over his head. Turning around, he saw that she stood behind him. He could see the shadow of the revolver in her hand, but heard her locking the safety on it. He had to admit he felt a sense of relief. "Romee, give me the gun back."

"I wasn't going to take it," she said after a moment of hesitation. He felt his gun laid in his hand and her hand pause on top of it. The silence between them lasted a moment longer before she dropped silently to the floor. "Turn on the lights," she whispered.

"What?"

"What would you normally be doing? Walking around in the dark? No. You'd turn on the lights. Get a drink from the fridge or whatever you do, head to your room, maybe shower, I don't know what you do, but do it. If it stays dark in here . . ."

"Gotcha. I was talking to my uncle . . ." Thinking of the cops outside, he thought about what he would be doing if she weren't there and quickly turned on the table lamp by the sofa and flopped on the sofa, clicking on the TV. "Okay, well, I'd unwind a bit in front of the TV," he mumbled. "They're looking all over for you. Why did you run?" he asked without looking at her.

She lay on her stomach on the floor. "I don't know, because it's all too freaky. Something just freaked me out . . . that woman, Hank and Aston. My God, Aston was gonna shoot me," she whispered excitedly, no doubt thinking of her colleague and someone she remotely called friend on occasion.

"Did you know that guy was a cop?" Keliegh asked.

Rolling on her back, she rested her arm over her eyes. She was fighting agitation, Keliegh could tell. "I'd never seen him before. Are you sure?"

"I'm sure." Keliegh replied.

"God . . . Well, what happened after I left?" she asked.

"At the scene, this big guy shows up and says, 'Okay, fellas, I'm with IA, get in the car.' So we did. It was weird, but we went to this place and got questioned—I didn't even get to go back to the station. Just told me I was suspended and that was that. Been trying to call the captain, but I can't get through."

"I thought for sure you would be in jail right now."

"Me too. But no."

"Some big guy at the scene . . . That seems funny, don't you think?"

"Yeah, sorta. He was some brotha I'd never heard of, Max-well something. Have you ever heard of him?"

"No, he must be new. But then again, I don't keep up with IA."

"I feel ya, but anyway he interrogated us for hours on end . . . But wanna hear something weird? I mean, I get sus-pended and Tommy hasn't even called me."

"You think she doesn't know?"

"How could she not know? I got suspended. It's been, like, two hours and who knows about Aston and Hank. I mean, that place was crawling with cop cars within seconds after you left. They practically shut the place down. Cops I'd never seen before—everywhere. They just showed up and cleaned up." Ke-liegh turned his head and looked at her. "It was like a movie . . . just weird. Oh, and I went by your place. It's trashed."

"What? My place is trashed? What were they looking for?"

Keliegh hesitated. He no longer cared about the losers out in the car stalking his house, the ones waiting to nab a good cop like Romia for something she didn't do. He stood and headed to his bedroom, clicking on the small lap by his bed. He came back to the living room and shut off the light, but not the TV. "Come on," he whispered, curling his finger for her to follow him into the dark hallway.

After reaching the hallway that had no windows, Romia stood, patting her pockets in order to feel her one prized pos-session taken earlier from her apartment. Earlier, Romia had made it to her apartment and snagged the tapestry from the frame that hung on her wall. Her apartment had been intact when she arrived. Surely she'd been tailed closely, but not closely enough. She'd spent about four minutes at her place. She'd changed her high-heeled boots to running shoes, pulled her hair under a beanie, and layered a black bodysuit under some loose black sweats and a white wifebeater.

The Shadow had inspired her outfit. She figured that if he could get into places covertly she'd better practice his technique, and so far it had worked. The dark clothing allowed her to pretty much just walk right past the officers staked out in the car, and on in through Keliegh's bedroom window. She thought about the small hole she'd made to unlatch the lock so she could crawl through. Perhaps it was her adrenaline pumping, but her actions and abilities had stunned even her a little bit.

"Somebody musta followed me to my place. I went there right after I left the streets. Tonight I had the weirdest experience." She paused and then shook her head as if suddenly not wanting to share any more with him. "Oh, yeah, I broke your window," she now confessed. Keliegh smiled sadly at her and, out of what seemed to be reflex, he stroked her cheek.

She knew Keliegh wanted her to talk to him, but she knew that she wouldn't. Maybe she couldn't. Maybe it was because she didn't have a clue what was going on either.

"What did your uncle say?"

Thinking of Lawrence Miller's words, Keliegh decided not to share what he was told. "What we gonna do, Rome?" he asked, abbreviating her name.

She shrugged, pulling off the beanie.

"You gotta turn yourself in."

"No, Keliegh, not until I know what's going on. Not until I find that woman and ask her why she lied. Not until—"

"Romia, I want to know all that too, but—"

Just then there was a knock at the door. Glancing at Romia standing in the windowless hallway now, wide-eyed and antsy, he held his hand up to assure her she would be safe. Dashing into the bathroom that too had no windows, he turned on the shower and pointed for her to go in, before quickly removing his shirt and heading to the door. Opening it, he saw Tommy standing there.

"Tommy, it's . . ." Keliegh looked at his watch.

"Two o'clock, I know," she said, brushing past him into the living room. "Hey, is your place being watched? What's going on?"

"Who called you?"

"Hank. Said Romia went off—kicked Aston's ass and tried to kill you and him both. Then she shot some guy. What's going on? Romia shot somebody? He said she's snapped—went nuts. Said she killed a cop?" Tommy looked around casually. He could see she noticed his revolver lying out in the open. That wasn't like him to leave it out like that, especially with the chamber out. He knew it. She knew it.

"She hasn't snapped. Everybody is always saying stuff like that about her. She's a little different but she's not . . . snappable," he said, hoping to keep his voice low enough for Tommy to hear but for Romia not to.

"Then why you got a bodyguard all of a sudden?" Tommy asked, partially sounding tongue-in-cheek. "You know she's gotta turn herself in. Hank said she's on the lam."

Romia was viewed as a strange bird on the force. Her upbringing in the foster home and "different" way of looking at life had her on the oddball list for sure. She was holistic and vegan. She only drank water, and although she carried a service revolver, she had never drawn it. Romia could kill in a matter of seconds with her bare hands in just one blow, and so had no need for a gun. She was pretty, wore high heels while on duty, and carried herself on the streets as if untouchable, yet mingling freely with the street life. Hardly ever smiling, no one could read her face and, therefore, she was a little intimidating and hated—maybe even feared. No one understood her except him, of that Keliegh was certain. He knew she had a soft side, a vulnerable side, and because of his feelings, he had decided a long time ago not to force it to the forefront. He never took their friendship any further than he felt the boundaries prevented. There were plenty of pigeons out there, there was no sense in trying to cage a—he thought about her helmet—a phoenix.

Tommy continued to wander around the living room. She was observant, and he knew she saw more than he wanted her to. "So where is she?" Tommy asked. She could hear the water running—Keliegh noticed her eyes dart in that direction.

"How would I know?" he asked coolly while sitting on the sofa.

"Weren't you about to shower?" she asked, noting his appearance and the sound of the wasting water. Tommy started for the hallway, and that's when she noticed Romia's black beanie on the floor.

"What the hell is this?" Tommy asked, picking it up, examining the long black hair that she pulled for it. "She's here!" Tommy started for the bathroom just as the water shut off.

"Tommy, stop!" Keliegh yelped, but it was too late. The door burst open and Romia came out swinging. Tommy blocked her first punch but was nailed by the second, slamming into the wall.

"Romia. No!" Tommy yelped, blocking the punches that came fast and furious. Tommy too had studied martial arts but was nowhere near Roma's skills set, as Tommy was more into kickboxing.

Suddenly, and with lightening speed, Romia had Tommy by the throat, pinned to the wall. Her hand rose, poised to strike a blow that could possibly kill. "Romia, no," Tommy whispered, grimacing while closing one eye, as if readying herself. "I want to help you. Let's go together . . . turn yourself in."

"I'm leaving, Tommy. I'm not turning myself in . . . not until I get some answers." Romia's words were final, ending with a blow that stunned Tommy, rendering her instantly unconscious. She dropped to the floor like a sack of potatoes.

Glancing once at Keliegh, who hesitated before stepping toward her, she grabbed her beanie while holding up her hand, indicating that he was in for a beat down too if he came any closer. Both of their eyes went to the crumbled heap of Tommy on the floor. "Tell her I'm sorry when she wakes up."

"You need some sleep."

"I may never sleep again, Keliegh," Romia promised. She began to unbutton Tommy's shirt.

"What are you doing?"

"Tommy just came in the front door and I'm leaving in her place. Don't try to stop me. I want to find out who trashed my place, who killed that man—better yet, who was that man—and who is trying to frame me for his murder."

Romia slid quickly from her black hoodie, dropping it to the floor before wrestling Tommy from her blouse, the heavy Western jacket with fringes, and cowboy hat that she was known to wear often. "But one thing I'm not doing. I'm not getting in them boots," she said after sliding into Tommy's blouse and shrugging into Tommy's jacket. Tucking the black hoodie into the pocket of the jacket, she pulled up her hair, fitted the hat square on her head, and headed to the door.

Keliegh followed, opening the door for her as he would if she were Tommy leaving. Raising his hand for a high five, which was apparently his and Tommy's common good-bye, he noticed the officer's eyes shift in their direction. "He's watching," Keliegh admonished.

"Good," Romia mouthed, heading for Tommy's car. Digging deep into the pocket, she luckily found Tommy's car keys, and climbing in, she slid behind the wheel. She didn't remove the hat, but drove right past the officer who simply waved in her direction. "Goombah," she mumbled.

Keliegh accepted that men—him included—just didn't notice women that closely, and that clown in the car apparently was not able to tell in the dark one tall, slender woman from another.

Walking back inside, he noticed Tommy sitting up in the hallway, holding the side of her head. She seemed discombobulated.

"She's gone. Thanks a lot, Tommy. Thanks a friggin' lot. Now she doesn't trust me. I could have maybe gotten her to turn herself in. This is going to be harder if she doesn't turn herself in!" Keliegh threw up his hands in frustration. "Dammit!"

"And, yeah, I'm okay too," Tommy groaned, holding the side of her head where Romia's blow had landed. "I probably have a damn concussion, but that's okay . . . it's okay. She got away, so it's all okay."

"Oh, stop whining. You don't have a concussion."

"And you care, I can tell," Tommy went on, before Keliegh held out his hand to help her to her feet.

"Oh, yeah, and you don't have a car, either," Keliegh added. "So you can't go home tonight. I'm sure she's at your place."

Looking down at herself, she noticed her camisole showing. "What the fu . . .?" Confusion covered her face. "Where is my jacket! And my hat! My blouse!"

"Oh, and you don't have any clothes, either," Keliegh added, changing his tone to a more sheepish one.

"Keliegh, damn! Well, if she isn't a murderer, she sure as hell is a thief."

Chapter 10

Trying not to fiddle with the keys too awfully much at Tommy's front door, Romia slid quickly inside. Pulling Tommy's hat and jacket off, she headed straight to the kitchen. Jerking open the fridge, she realized her hunger when spying Tommy's array of assorted snacks. She pulled out the Chinese takeout container and gave it a sniff; the rankness wriggled her nostrils. The pizza box was filled with vileness too. Tossing it back in, she pulled out the bag of almonds. "Yeah, this'll work." Looking again through the veggie drawer, she found some barely alive carrots and a bag of leftover pre-washed salad. Quickly, she threw a naked salad together, sprinkling it with the almonds, and began to scarf it down. She was starving, but stopped eating after several mouthfuls. She knew she'd better eat light and get her body used to sporadic eating until she at least spent a day investigating this killing. She'd have to be light on her feet and ready for flight, or maybe even fight, at any given moment. Someone was framing her and she had to get to the bottom of it. She had to find out who this Shadow was, too; just the thought of him holding her helmet hostage chapped her hide. Digging in her bra, she pulled out the folded tapestry and opened it. "Yeah, he's gotta be the first to go if anybody is going out in this game!"

Glancing at the clock, she saw that it was four A.M. Surely Keliegh had kept Tommy at his place. Common sense would have told him to, right? He'd have to know, having Tommy there would buy her a few hours. If not, and Tommy showed

up, then she'd have to do what she had to do. There was no
way she was turning herself in right now . . . not without answers.

Romia sat in Tommy's large swivel recliner, her mind drifting to the previous night's events. Everything was moving so
fast. Internal Affairs was already on her tail. "Maxwell something. I'll need to give him a call and start some negotiations,"
Romia thought out loud as her mind lifted. "The Shadow.
Who the heck is that guy?" she asked the air. "Why does he
seem so familiar? I must know him. He seems to know me. He
is the key to this whole thing. Who trashed my place? What
did they want?" she asked, squiggling deeper into the large
chair. Her eyes weighed a ton, and she knew if she closed
them it was all over. She shook her head. "I should get some
cold water," she said, glancing over the back of the chair toward the kitchen—it seemed so far away. "I'll get some in a
minute.

"Okay, why would that woman want to frame me? Who
was the guy in the bar? Okay, so he was a cop . . . God, he
was a cop?" Romia covered her face. A second later she was
jerking her head awake. She'd been asleep for an hour. Jumping to her feet, she looked around for her hoodie that she'd
tucked under the jacket and tossed to the side when she came
into Tommy's apartment. Sliding out of Tommy's blouse, she
folded it, laid it on the arm of the sofa, and slid into her own
clothing.

Thinking about the day and what it might hold, she rum-
maged around Tommy's kitchen until she found a water
bottle, and filled it with water from the hot/cold dispenser.
She revisited the bag of almonds and then, on second thinking, she put the entire bag in her pocket. "I owe you," she
mumbled. "No, you're one crazy chick, challenging me like
that! What is your crazy problem? I could have been sleeping
in Keliegh's bed right now, safe and sound! No. You flippin'

owe me!" Romia reasoned. She stopped and thought about the words that just crossed her lips. "What am I thinking? I gotta get outta here. Why do people always think about sex at times like this?"

Romia looked over her shoulder every now and then, feeling the peering eyes of a watcher. She could only think about the Shadow. *But how could he know where I am?* she asked herself, shaking off the thought of something so ridiculous. She had to find answers. Surely, Mike, the bartender, would have some answers for her about the woman. *Even if I have to beat the answers out of him*, she thought, chuckling to herself. That had never been her style, but in the last few hours she'd come to realize that sometimes people only cooperated when they felt threatened . . . *or they're unconscious*, she added, thinking about Tommy. Striking out on foot, she hurried to the bus stop. She'd pay Tommy back her change when she saw her again.

"She just left Tamika Turner's place," the Shadow reported.

"Follow her. I want to know what she does next. I want to see exactly how she plans to get out of this situation. I need to know how she reasons under pressure."

"So far she's acting like . . . Sheesh, she's standing at a bus stop like . . . like she's not a wanton felon. She's acting like a . . . like a girl."

"She is a girl, in case you haven't noticed."

"I noticed." The Shadow chuckled wickedly, starting the engine on Romia's Ducati motorcycle.

Chapter 11

About fifteen years ago

She sat in the restaurant. Her heart was beating harder than ever before. A reunion formed from the betrayal of a mutual friend had its mixed emotions. To trust or not to trust was the question.

Did he trust her? Maybe not . . .

But she loved him. With all her being, she loved him.

Glancing at the clock, she saw that it grew late. "He's not coming," she told herself, speaking in French, in an undertone. It had been many years since she'd spoken in her native tongue and tonight she realized it indeed sounded foreign, even to her own ears.

She'd worked hard to disguise her accent, until finally she believed it to be gone. The waiter brought her second glass of sparkling wine. They called it champagne, but only in Paris could one get a decent glass of champagne. Here in America . . .

She sighed heavily, thinking about France, Egypt, Morocco, Germany, Copenhagen, New York City, all the places she'd lived before settling in this small town, before giving in to her paranoia and overworked nervous system. She was tired.

Running her hand through her thick blond hair, she pulled some strands through her fingers to where she could see them in front of her. For so many years she had been blond, having given up her rich brown tresses right after giving birth. Her green eyes too were now blue—changed by contacts. So much effort to put forth in developing a new life when, in fact, so few knew she was alive, and of those few, only two really mattered.

The air grew thick now in this restaurant. So thick it took her breath away. Looking around desperately, she attempted to find the source of her distraction. It had to be him. "Why don't I see him?" she mumbled, straining and craning her neck.

There was a woman who caught her eye. She was black and very lovely as were her features and full her body. She was truly Nubian in every sense of the word. Her passion spoke before her lips even moved. She was captivating. Capri could only stare, for, suddenly, she realized the man who sat down at the table with her . . .

It is he.

He had arrived. It was just as she had been told. He always came here. *How foolish he is to frequent such a public place,* she reasoned. The lump in her throat was hard to swallow. She could only take in air, unable to breathe it out.

When he kissed the woman, she felt it on her own cheek and touched her face there. He kissed her quickly again on the lips and there Capri felt the second burn. That was when he, too, felt her presence. She was sure of it, as he looked around cautiously, his steel grey eyes scanning the room quickly. She sat tall in her seat, waiting for his gaze to come her way, but it did not. It stopped short at another table. The couple at that table, noticing him, stood and welcomed him over, loudly expressing their happiness to see him. They called his name—a name Capri had never heard before.

"Boss Man! You and Niema come here often?"

"All the time," he answered as he and the beautiful woman, who must have been Niema stood from their table to join them. The waiter helped move their glasses and table settings.

He said something to the waiter as they moved to the next table. It was spoken behind the woman's back, but she caught the exchange.

The restaurant was comfortable enough for Capri to sit there for over an hour, watching the four of them talk, eat, laugh, and pay their tab and leave. Never once did he look her way. They walked out of the restaurant as happy as when they'd arrived.

Her heart weighed a ton.

Gathering her purse, she stood to leave. The waiter came up to her table with a tray that held one single glass of red wine. "Oh, yes, I do owe for the time I spent taking up room here." She smiled, reaching into her bag. The waiter held up his hand and slid the glass from the tray onto the table in front of her.

"A gentleman bought this for you and told me to give you this," the waiter said, holding out his hand. On his palm sat a small pebble. Capri's heart leapt as she hungrily grabbed the stone and clutched it to her chest. "He also paid your tab."

"Do you know that man? Do you know his name?"

"No. I'm sorry. I'm new here—most of us on staff tonight are fairly new. He appears to be a regular but, I'm sorry, I don't know him. He paid cash, so there is no way of finding out who he was tonight."

"It's all right. I think I know who he was . . ."

"Well, drink up and have a good night, ma'am," the waiter said, spinning on his heels and walking away.

Capri sat back at the table and got comfortable again. She sipped the wine slowly, allowing all the pain, joy, and memories fade into the throat of it. It was rich French wine—not unlike a taste from home.

Chapter 12

Back to the story

Tommy woke up in Keliegh's bed. She looked around, gathering her bearings. "That's right, he's on the sofa," she mumbled, still half asleep, but fully disappointed. She had on his T-shirt and sweats, thanks to Romia mugging her the night before.

Swinging her long legs over the side of the bed, she sat up and stretched. Keliegh's bed was more than comfy. *If only he had shared it*, she thought, allowing her mind to wander into the forbidden place for half a second before snapping back to reality.

Her head throbbed. She suddenly remembered the beating she had taken from Romia. "Crazy chick! You owe me big time," she mumbled, again under her breath.

After a pit stop at the bathroom to take the sleep off and all that, she shuffled into the living room, finding Keliegh on the sofa, scouring the newspaper.

"Nothing," he barked, flipping the paper over as if maybe planning to go through it again, a little closer this time.

"Excuse me," she grumbled, thinking, hoping, praying he had coffee. With a girlfriend like Shashoni, he should have had all sorts of goodies because . . . *baby has back and loves to eat . . .* from what she had seen at the last precinct party. Shashoni put a hurting on that appetizer tray. Tommy ventured into Keliegh's kitchen and, sure enough, the coffee pot, and some bear claws were right there waiting. *Perfection! Gotta love a thick girlfriend*, Tommy thought. Okay, so Shashoni actually had a perfect hourglass shape, but still, when one was tall and skinny like she was, everyone was thicker . . . well, except Romia. *Now, that chick is stoked. She probably less than 1 percent body fat. She's like a machine*, Tommy thought now, remembering again the speed of Romia's punches. Tommy was a third-level black belt and champion kickboxer, but still she would hate to meet Romia in competition. *That chick is off this planet. She's got some secret-weapon kinda moves 'n' shit*, Tommy internally admired.

"Nothing about a cop killing. Nothing about Romia being on the run. Nothing on TV. No APBs, nothing . . ."

"You going in today?" Tommy asked after getting the coffee pot humming and the pastry arranged on a plate.

"No. I'm suspended, remember?"

"Maybe you're not," Tommy said, sounding almost nonchalant. "Hank is a liar . . . an idiot, too. Cap'n didn't say anything to me when I bolted outta there, like, 'Stop her, he's suspended.'"

"Well, that's what Maxwell What's-His-Name told me. So . . ."

Tommy and Keliegh shared a moment of silence, as if both collecting their next thoughts and questions. "I wonder what happened to Shoni."

"You want me to go check out her place?"

"No, I'll go. I mean, damn, one would think the cops would have done that and she would have been there at the inquiry—or something. Maybe they did. Maybe they trashed her place like they trashed Romia's."

Tommy turned toward him, jumping up backward on the counter next to the coffee pot. "Why would anybody trash Shashoni's place? That's dumb. Why would anybody trash

Romia's? I mean, maybe it's not as dumb as trashing Shoni's place, but, like, when would anybody have had time if they were questioning you?" She then took a big bite from her pastry.

"Well, somebody did. It was mad trashed."

"Okay, Keliegh, let's start over. What happened and what are we going to do about it? You know I'm up for it. You had my back when all that happened with my best friend and her daughter last year, so now I'll help you with Romia. If you swear to me you believe she's innocent, I swear to you I'll help you . . . despite her kicking my ass last night."

"You had that ass kickin' coming, but yeah, I know she's innocent."

Tommy rolled her eyes. "How do you figure? But anyway . . ."

"Don't even start," Keliegh said before breaking into laughter.

"Okay, I don't go in until tonight, so what do you need me to do today?"

Keliegh walked into the kitchen, took the pastry from Tommy's hand, and shoved the last bite into his mouth. He looked at her for a long time, as if wondering where to start. "Okay, let me sum up as best I can," he began, as if attempting to relive an unbelievable dream or a nightmare and unsure of which.

"Okay, so where do we start?"

"Well, I think if we know who got killed, then we can start figuring out why that man needed to die."

"And why he needed Romia to kill him," Tommy added, starting on a second pastry.

Chapter 13

Romia reached The Spot—the tavern where everything had gone down just a few hours prior. There was no caution tape and no sign of police activity. It wasn't open, but there were a couple of cars parked in the lot. She looked the cars over from a distance to see if, perhaps, any were unmarked police cars. But none met the description. Looking around, she searched for any immediate hints or clues that might lead her to answers about the night before. "Somebody died here, for crying out loud. There should be signs or indications," she mumbled under her breath. There wasn't so much as a chalk outline, or even blood stains in the dirt . . . not even her own.

Feeling odd about things, she pushed the door open and eased into the bar, quickly skimming the room. There were only two or three people there—employees apparently—and Mike, the owner and bartender. Pulling the hood from her head, she slid up on a stool and waited for him to turn around. When he did, she marked his expression. It was one of surprise.

"What are you doing here, Romee? I thought you'd be in jail or out of the country." His voice was an undertone; it was obvious he was trying to be discreet.

"Not me. Maybe that woman who shot that man here last night . . . but not me." She glanced around. Mike handed her a small bottle of mineral water instead of pouring it into a glass. Accepting it, she turned the cap and took a swig. "I figured you'd be closed up tighter than a drum."

"Not me. Cops did what they had to do last night and that was that."

"Really, and what was it exactly that they did? A man died outside your business and it doesn't appear they did much."

"Well, I didn't kill him, so . . ."

"Neither did I. That woman . . ."

"What woman, Romee?" he asked, rubbing a tumbler dry. "You keep saying that."

"What woman? Mike, what . . . ?" Romia sighed and shook her head in disbelief of his comment. "The woman who was screaming bloody murder and accusing me of the same. Surely, your memory can't be that short," Romia whispered, leaning in close to his face.

"Oh, that woman," Mike said, chuckling nervously, redrying the same tumbler as if his mind and actions were no longer working as one. "Romia, I've never seen her before. I noticed her when she came in. She was new. I watched her for a while, ya know, just making sure she wasn't a hooker or anything like that. Can't have that kind of trash in here stirring up trouble. Anyway, I watched her and it was like she was waiting for somebody, okay? Then you came in and all that ruckus with Shoni and Kel and then boom. I look up; everybody is outside and there's been a shooting."

"Did you hear a shot? Did the woman come back in?"

"I swear. She didn't come back in. She never came back in. By the time I got everybody outta here, she was not one of them."

"Where did she go?"

Mike splayed his fingers in the air as if imitating a mist dissipating. "It was like a ghost. She was gone."

"Damn!" Romia spat. Mike was a little taken aback by her language. Romia wasn't one to curse.

"How is Keliegh? He got carted off so fast I figured he was going to jail too."

"Nothing happened to him . . . I guess."

"Good. Would hate to see his career all messed up over . . ." Mike paused. Looking Romia straight in the eyes, he asked, "Did you shoot that guy, Romee? I mean, everybody is saying you did. That IA guy said you did. He called you a swerve."

"Swerve? What is that?"

"Like a disgruntled postal worker, I guess. You know, a cop who finally snaps. You never heard the term? I never heard the term."

"Never needed to know the term, and no, I haven't snapped." Romia felt her blood beginning to boil. This was the second time she'd heard her mental state being questioned. Tommy had said something about it last night and now Mike was inquiring. Was everyone thinking she was crazy? She sure was starting to feel that way. Crazy.

"Romia, everybody knows your temper. Your jacket got messed up with that little Jack Daniels and you . . . you got out of control and shot that guy . . . for nothing. It was your gun that killed him, I heard," Mike added, looking around. "And now you're on the lam. And, actually, I think you need to leave here before you bring the heat on me for real. That Maxwell guy said he'd have my license if I even 'thought out loud' about last night, let alone talk about it with anybody."

"Mike, come on, you know I didn't shoot that guy. For what. Bumping me—"

"Yeah, just like that. He got booze on that fancy jacket of yours and you lost it."

Smacking her lips, she readied her mouth to deny it, but then surrendered without a fight. "Yeah, well. Did you know him?"

"No. Just like that woman. Had never seen either of them before."

"Dang, Mike, do better than that, gimmie something."

"I can't. That guy talked to me, Romia. I can't talk to any-body about anything. He'll pull my liquor license and—"

"What guy?"

"The IA guy, Max . . ."

"Maxwell something. Yeah, been hearing that name a lot. Mike, you know everybody in this precinct and beyond. Who is that guy? Keliegh doesn't know him. I don't know him."

"Never seen him before either, but he's good—new, I guess. But whatever he is, he got this place cleaned up in record time. Got that body outta here, questioned everybody, and, well . . . took care of it. I'm supposed to call him, ya know, if by chance I see you."

"So you knew I wasn't in jail." Romia sighed before look-ing around and then back at Mike. His eyes twinkled with the sparkle of a bad little boy. "So . . . have you seen me?" she asked, almost smiling, but not.

"Not by chance." Mike grinned, reaching down and sliding her the card that carried Maxwell's phone number.

"Thanks, Mike." Romia stood, patting the bar consolingly as if it were a longtime friend. "Mike. Believe it or not, I have an alibi."   •

"You do?"

"Yeah, but I can't tell you right now, it's even crazier than thinking I shot that guy." Romia chuckled slightly.

Just then the door opened behind her. Mike looked over her head. "Morning, officers," he called out loud. Romia didn't turn around, but readied herself for whatever might happen next. Slowly, she pulled the hood of her sweat jacket over her head. Mike's eyes met hers and she doubted for just a second whether he would be loyal to her. His smile, however, gave her the answer. She eased to the side as they approached the bar.

"So you know we're cops?" one of the men asked. His Eng-lish was good, but his accent was foreign.

"Been serving cops for years. Know 'em a mile away."

"Good. Then I guess you know the cop we're looking for. Romia Smith. We heard she hangs out here. Have you seen her?" the other of the two men said, sounding flat. Both men had an accent that Romia wasn't sure at first she recognized. It was familiar, but for the life of her, if she'd ever heard it before it had been years. Maybe it was one of her mother's friends who spoke as this man did. She couldn't remember.

Romia was dying to look at him but she knew she'd better get out of there. Her coming back to the scene of the crime was not what normally would have been expected, even she knew that. Only on television did the perps come back to the murder scene . . . *unless they are psychopaths and just dropping in to watch the fire.* The thought made her suddenly swoon. *Maybe I am crazy,* she reasoned. *Swerved . . .*

"Why would she do that?" Mike asked. "This would be the last place she'd come. You fellas must be new around here."

"You could say that," one of the men said before chuckling.

Romia moved away from the bar and on through the tavern toward the door, but before she could get out, the door opened and a third man walked in. The man was dressed in a business suit, complete with a tie that was clipped with a unique-looking clip. He was big and dark skinned, sporting a shiny ring loaded with gaudy-looking stones. He didn't look like any plainclothes cop she'd seen recently. Their eyes met for one second before he yelled out something in another language. It sounded . . . *French, maybe. A dialect . . . maybe Arabic.*

Arabic? she thought, wondering why that came to her mind.

Suddenly swinging on her, she blocked him and countered with a punch-and-kick combo, but he blocked, coming back with the same. Despite his attire, he was agile and skilled in martial arts—a mixture of many skill levels and different schools. The fight was on and, by all appearances, about to get vicious.

The employees cleaning tables backed out of the way as the two of them fought around the room. With one of his hard punches, Romia tumbled over one of those clean tables, landing on her feet. His grace was gone then as he turned into a wrestler straight from the WWE, picking Romia up and throwing her onto the stacked-up chairs in the corner. She hit them hard and rolled onto the floor, covering her head for protection from the crashing fold-up chairs, but was back on her feet within seconds. The two other men joined in, but were not as challenging as the big guy in the fancy threads. With a side kick to the face, Romia knocked one of the men out cold. But the other one swung on her, catching her off guard. She avoided a face punch, however. The big guy stepped closer and now she was cornered against the wall.

"You fellas have names?" she asked. Her fists were up to protect her face. She was breathing hard but far from ready to surrender. "Or is that a secret you plan to take to your grave?"

"Ha! You and your cocky attitude . . . just like your father," the big guy said, smiling broadly. "You truly are a phoenix."

Confusion filled Romia's brain. She thought of the tapestry piece taken from the frame, the beautiful handcrafted stitchery that depicted the redivivus bird. "Phoenix? My father?" Noticing the fists of the big guy, she saw the ring up close. "Phoenix?" she asked.

"Don't play coy. We know who you are—but clearly you won't live to know as much," the smaller man said, flipping out a switchblade. The larger one looked at him, and then pulled out a larger knife, showing his compliance with the plan to slice and dice over the first plan of just pummeling her to death.

"So, I'm starting to think you're not the police," Romia said, sarcasm dripping from her lips. She felt at home in this battle and was ready to take it to the death.

"Hey!" Mike called out, rising from behind the bar with his

gun pointed. But the smaller man's aim shut off Mike's voice and ended his intent.

The young female employee was still in the bar area. She had been standing against the wall, paralyzed with fear until that moment. She screamed, seeing the switchblade sticking from Mike's throat.

The smaller man drew his gun then, and took aim at the screaming girl.

Romia's instincts were instantaneous. She went for the gun, snapping the man's wrist in the process. He screamed in pain but was silenced when Romia, in one movement, broke his neck. She used him as a shield to block the inward jab of the larger man's blade. In a fluid motion, she moved him in front of her just in time. The blade went through his arm, catching the fabric of her hoodie, cutting the fabric, nicking her skin.

"Come on!" the young man yelled, coming from the back room where he had taken cover. He ran out, pulled the young female to him, and slammed the back door of the bar, making their escape.

Romia was livid. She could no longer see straight. Visions of her mother's smile were all that filled her eyes now. *"Romia,"* her mother called. *"Slow down, honey. Faster isn't always best. You could get hurt, and you know Mother would be devastated if something happened to her little heartbeat."* she said.

The tapestry flashed before Romia's eyes now, as the voice repeated the words. *My little heartbeat . . . slow down . . . your father . . . the Phoenix . . . you don't know who you are.*

The car barreling toward them was all Romia could see, as her mind went back in time. "Mama!" she screamed out . . . then and now!

As if suddenly possessed, Romia's rage was taken out on the big man. Combinations of her immediate conception came to her with remarkable quickness. Again and again she pummeled the man's face and chest, taking his breath away until finally a slice from the side of her hand to his throat caused him to gasp and choke. Blood spurted forth from his open mouth from a swift kick to his chest. He stumbled backward, but Romia didn't stop there. She kicked high, reaching his chin. The sound of the man's bones cracking under her foot sickened her—much like the sound of her mother going over the hood of that car.

He fell, bleeding from his mouth and nose, his face resembling a prize fighter's. He was dead.

Without a doubt, Romia figured real cops were coming. But it didn't matter at that moment, not really. Out of instinct, though, she quickly rifled through their jackets for ID. She found none. Regardless of who they were, there would be no way the authorities who headed her way would understand her side of things. There was no way they would believe that she had not killed Mike, instead of having killed on Mike's behalf.

Rushing out the back door, she thought her eyes were playing tricks on her. Her Ducati with her helmet hanging from the bungee sat waiting. "My God!" she screamed, rushing toward her bike. She wanted to hug it, kiss it as she would a lost love, but instead she mounted it, slammed her helmet on her head, and took off.

"They're here and they found her. We're out of time now," the Shadow said in Arabic, running while talking on the small transmission device. He was headed toward the freeway overpass.

"Dammit! How did they find her?"

"I don't know, but they beat me here. I suppose after tearing up her apartment they decided to use their brains instead of their brawn. So whatever game you were playin' with her, it just got stepped up a notch."

"God, yes, to level ten. We're gonna have to pull her in."

"Like that's going to be easy. She's scared. She doesn't even realize what she's done."

"Doesn't matter. Use whatever means at your disposal to get her to me."

"At least she's mobile again. I gave her back the bike."

"And you?"

"I'm not concerned with me . . . nobody is. Remember, I'm already dead," he said, a sick chuckle following his words. Closing the transmission by tapping the end button on his wrist band, he watched the cars passing under the overpass until finally he saw his chance. He leapt to his escape, landing in the open trailer of a large, slow-moving truck that was right on time.

Chapter 14

The Coroner's Office

Yes, it was a great place to start. Keliegh was a good investigator—so was Romia, for that matter. She had detective in her blood but never wanted it. A few years younger than him, she was happy working a beat. She said it kept her close to the earthlings. "Hmmm." Keliegh pondered her words for a moment, and then laughed at what her comment implied about the rest of the police force.

Keliegh had called the station to speak with the chief, but found him unavailable, again. "Of course. Press conference. Big time," Keliegh reasonably assumed. Turning onto Grand Boulevard, he headed to the morgue in the Palemos precinct. The body was not in the morgue his precinct used, so he was certain now that the Palemos guys had the collar. He had no idea why his uncle was still playing dumb about last night's shooting, but then again, maybe he truly didn't know everything. The coroner on the scene would have taken the body to this morgue if, indeed, Palemos guys had the case. If nothing else, he'd get a chance to check in with his uncle again if the body was here.

"And it would explain why I didn't know any of those cats," he told Tommy when she checked in.

"Make sense. I'll call in a couple of favors and see who caught the whistle over there, since your uncle didn't know,"

Tommy assured him. "Oh, and I got called in, so I'm on to-night. I'll ask around fa sho then about your suspension."

"Thanks," Keliegh hung up.

A call to his uncle was now in order. "Hey, uncle," Keliegh greeted his Uncle Lawrence.

"Funny you should call. I was going to call you. So, you a soothsayer now? Seems ya former partner has lost her damn mind a little bit. How'd you predict it?"

"Predict it? You can't predict what has already occurred."

"Yeah, but how did you know?"

"What are you talking about? You're talking like something *just* happened."

"It did. I'm here now, wading through a wheelbarrow full of dead bodies. So, is she on some kinda killing spree or what?"

"What the hell are you talking about?"

"I'm at this tavern you folks visit. Seems your partner did some killing up in here about an hour ago."

"What? No. She's being framed for what happened last night. I don't have a clue what happened this morning."

"I don't know anything about last night. I just know that about an hour ago, she just showed up here and murdered a bartender and three early-morning patrons. We got a call from some pretty scared employees who saw it all go down."

"What?"

"Look. I'm no judge, and thank the Lord I'm not on the jury, but your girl is a swerve—pure and simple. We got witnesses say she came in and did a slice and dice . . . no nice."

"Well, they're lying!" Keliegh yelled. "I'm telling you. Romia didn't do it."

"You give me a bit more than just your word and I'll listen a bit harder, okay? But for now, I'm cleaning up your ex's dirty work. Won't take but a minute to get the DA to issue a warrant and my chief to put out an APB on your girl—"

"Wait! Don't do it, uncle. Let me get over there and—"

"Today I'm not your uncle. I'm a cop doing my job, Kel, and . . ." Lawrence inhaled heavily as he often did when on a crime scene. He had a weak stomach for blood. His heavy sigh told Keliegh all he needed to know about what his uncle was seeing. It had to be pretty bloody. "It's ugly here," Lawrence then confirmed.

"Okay. Okay," Keliegh stammered. "Look, I know you won't believe this, but last night this guy got shot right there at the same tavern."

"What!"

"That's what I was saying."

"Nothing happened here last night. There was no indication that anything happened here last night. The witnesses didn't say anything about a shooting last night."

"I was there. But I mean . . ." Keleigh ran his hand over his smooth waves. "Hell, I can't find the body. It's like it never happened. The guy she supposedly killed isn't in our morgue and you didn't even know about it. So I'm here now wondering if he's in your morgue."

"Probably not. I mean, if we got this call, we'da got last night's call too. But let me know if you find him. Pretty damn freaky."

"Who are the victims?"

"Victims? Besides the bartender, Mike, we have no idea."

"You're sure it's Mike?"

"Yeah, that much I know for sure."

"Damn," Keliegh sighed. "Okay, okay. Give me a minute before you call in the big dogs on Romia. Those witnesses . . . they're lyin'."

"Keliegh, I don't know, they said it was Romia. They know her."

"They are lying. I swear it."

"Bring Romia in," Lawrence said, sounding flat and cool. Keliegh knew his uncle and knew he wasn't gonna budge on that decision. Keliegh also knew he had only a short time to do it. Lawrence Miller was a straight-and-narrow cop. As soon as his ink dried on his report, he would be on his way to the DA's office, and that would be the end of Romia.

"Okay," Keliegh reluctantly agreed before hanging up.

Keliegh walked into the coroner's office. The receptionist was sitting at her station. He flashed his badge. "I'm Detective Jack, South City Homicide, here for the case of the John Doe who came in last night—shooting near the Palemos—a place call The Spot."

The receptionist quickly looked through her files. "Nothing," she answered mindlessly, cracking her gum. She looked bored.

"Well, maybe he got a name between the scene and here. Who was on the shift last night?"

"Me. And, no, nothing came in here last night. Nothing . . . like I said."

"I know the Palemos is a busy place on a Saturday night, but this guy was white and—"

"Don't care if he was purple. We had no Does, no Dids, nobody came in last night. Actually, we had a slight miracle last night. Nobody was shot and killed in the Palemos. Can you believe that?" She was shocked and her facial expression reflected that. "Stabbed, poisoned, and even a hari-kari, but no shootings."

"You are so wrong, because I was there!" Keliegh popped off, sounding argumentative and ready to dispute the matter.

The woman rolled her eyes and smacked her gum, popping a small bubble.

Just then, Maxwell Huntington appeared from the elevator that spilled into the lobby. He was talking to another man whom Keliegh didn't recognize. There was something fishy about Maxwell Huntington, and Keliegh wanted to figure this guy out. He didn't seem like a regular IA guy. He was slick and well groomed, controlled and, well, shady. He seemed to show up at the right time at all the wrong places . . . wrong as far as Keliegh was concerned. Like now. *What is he doing at the morgue?*

"You wanna look at my register? I mean, I don't miss dead bodies and I would have seen him if he had come in." The woman at the counter was getting loud, much to Keliegh's chagrin, because Maxwell looked up from his conversation with the shorter man he walked with.

"Detective Jack, what brings you among the dead?" he asked. Keliegh tried to think fast on his feet. Admitting that Romia had brought him there might not be the right thing to say.

"I was just . . . I mean, I was making sure that . . ."

"You're suspended. I suspended you. Why are you here? You waiting to get a look at the other men your partner murdered?" Maxwell barked the question. "They should be here any minute."

"You know, about that suspension, my partner didn't seem to know that I was suspended. I thought it odd that—"

"Under the circumstances, I wouldn't think you would want your colleagues to know how close you came to an obstruction charge and a few nights in jail. I've managed to work with your chief to keep this all pretty quiet . . . well, until this morning. Now it's outta my hands," he said, raising his hands as if in surrender.

"Oh, so I was looking at an obstruction charge, huh?" asked Keliegh, his brow furrowing. "And how in the world are you keeping it quiet when Ro . . . ?" He wanted to challenge Huntington further but the questions wouldn't come, not in light of what his uncle had just told him. "So what are you charging Romia Smith with?"

"Your ex-partner is a killer, or are you blind and stupid? It was all over the news this morning . . . breaking news. Romia

Smith is a killer." Maxwell's lips curved into a wicked grin.
"So what do you think we're gonna get the DA to charge her
with? And if you know where she is, I suggest you tell me,"
Maxwell requested.

His bluntness caught Keliegh off guard. "Why would you
think I'd know?"

"Because of your relationship."

"Relationship?"

"You used to be partners, moron. Unless there's more you
didn't tell me about?"

"Oh," Keliegh said then, trying to hide his guilt over having
seen Romia last night. "No, there's nothing more," he lied.

Maxwell looked around and then back at Keliegh. He licked
his full lips and lowered his voice. "Look, I know there's more.
I know there is," he said. "But listen to me . . . I also think
Romia might be innocent."

"Innocent. You think she's innocent. Since when, man?
You all but sent out a lynching party last night . . . and now?
Now with what's just happened, you expect me to believe you
and everyone else aren't out for blood?"

"Romia is in danger, in case you haven't noticed. And I'm
trying to help her."

"Danger? I thought she was dangerous. Make up your
mind."

"She's apparently snapped and I need to reel her in. She's
on a rampage. We suspect some revenge-type activity. We
think maybe it has to do with her mother's murder. We have
reason to believe that Romia is out for vengeance. The man
she shot at the bar last night was involved in her mother's
death. Didn't she tell you that?"

"What the hell! She never told me . . ." Keliegh attempted
to catch his words up with his thoughts so as not to say more
than he wanted to. "Her mother died when she was a kid."

"Sorry, I thought you knew. Her mother was murdered

three years ago. Perhaps you don't know Romia as well as you
thought you did. Romia is trained in martial arts with skills
to reach a deadly level. You thought she was doing this for
the police department's benefit. No, but for her own vigilante
mission. She's been using the police force as a resource to locate the people responsible for killing her mother. She's killed
five men in less than twenty-four hours and—"

"What? You're crazy. Romia doesn't even know what's going on."

"So you have heard from her?"

"No," Keliegh lied bold faced and stared at the IA man,
Maxwell Huntington. He held his lie solid until finally Maxwell realized he would not take it back.

"Fine! But be warned, Detective Jack. That woman is not
who you think she is. She's a vicious killer—an assassin. If
you had done your homework, you'd know what I'm talking
about. But for now, just know that if you get in her way, you
can expect to die next."

"She would never hurt me."

"Oh, no? I'm sure the bartender Mike, that 'friend' of hers,
thought the same thing."

"She didn't kill Mike."

Maxwell shrugged again, allowing a wicked grin to cross his
lips. Keliegh realized then that the man with him earlier had
walked off. "I wouldn't chance it," Maxwell said, bringing his
attention back to their conversation. "She's bent. Gone."

Keliegh knew in his heart he didn't believe any of this, yet
just hearing it was making him uncomfortable. Why hadn't
Romia told him her mother had been murdered? "Where is
the body from last night? I want to know his name. I want to
know who she supposedly killed today. And, yeah, how did
you know so fast? My uncle just got there and—"

"Oh, we've had our eyes on her. Make no mistake about
that." Maxwell shook his finger in Keliegh's face. "And when

we catch her, she's goin' down. And you listen good, mister, you are suspended. Go home. Go on vacation. Get outta our way, because if we keep tripping over your ass, you're going down too."

"You'll never catch her," Keliegh said, giving the receptionist who had gotten interested in their conversation an irritated look.

"Don't bet on it," Maxwell said.

Just then the phone rang. The receptionist answered it.

"You must be bad luck, mister. Now we got four bodies coming in all at once. Sheesh!" the receptionist called out. "As if my job isn't hard enough, gotta log in this stuff," she mumbled, focusing on her computer screen as if waiting for electronic confirmation of her phone call.

Keliegh turned back and looked at Maxwell, who smiled and shrugged.

"And I bet they have assassination written on all over them in bold letters—Romia Smith."

"Not everybody who dies in this city has Romia's name on them."

"Again, Mr. Bad Luck," Maxwell chuckled, repeating the receptionist, "don't bet on it!" Maxwell pushed Keliegh back and quickly headed back toward the elevator, as if he wanted to be the first to see the bodies that were coming in. Still, Keliegh looked around for the other man that was talking with Maxwell earlier, but he was gone.

Stepping outside, Keliegh thought about Romia. He needed to talk to her. He needed to believe her—to clear out from his head all Maxwell had said. Just then the phone rang. It was Tommy.

"Whatcha got?" he asked Tommy.

"Not much, but then, maybe a lot," she answered.

"What the hell does that mean?"

"Don't bite my head off. I'm stepping out on a limb here and maybe worse. I'm not even getting a thanks."

"Thanks," Keliegh barked.

"And you're welcome too."

"Sorry, it's that Maxwell Huntington guy. He was here at the morgue. The body wasn't here, but he was."

"Really? Wow, this is getting really interesting."

"I wouldn't call it interesting . . . not really." Keliegh responded.

"I would . . . 'cause nobody's heard of the guy. I keep trying to corner the captain but can't get near him." Tommy said.

"Who the hell is he?" Keliegh asked, turning back to the morgue doors, debating if he would go back in and find out on his own.

"Want another mystery? I was doing some snooping around, you know, seeing who's on this case and well, nobody is. That means nobody's heard of this Maxwell cat or a shooting last night. I wouldn't be surprised if you weren't suspended either. Hold on . . ."

Keliegh could hear the commotion through the muted phone. "You hear that? Captain stormed through asking what the hell was going on. He asked where you were. He said, 'Mike's dead?' This is like a sick joke."

"No joke. Apparently, somebody is claiming that Romia took out some guys at The Spot about an hour ago. For real. One of them was Mike."

"She killed Mike? Is that what all the hubbub is about? Things are getting really nutty around here. Mike is dead? Hey, wait a sec . . . who knew before we did?"

"Maxwell," they said at the same time.

"I'ma see if I can find out more about this Maxwell dude, maybe find out his game. Then I'm headed out to The Spot."

"I'll meet you there. Hey, what about your girlfriend?" Tommy said, allowing plenty of sarcasm to come through. "I mean, she just dropped outta sight and that's not like her."

Keliegh sighed heavily and hung up. "Oh, don't I know it. I still need to go see her."

After storming back into the morgue, Keliegh was told that Maxwell and his partner were gone. "How? I didn't see them leave." he asked the receptionist.

"Guess what? Apparently there is more than one way outta here, Mr. Bad Luck!"

"Hey, by the way, who all came in last night? I'll just take the entire roster."

"Ah, well, this I can tell you. Mr. Huntington told me not to tell you anything else. So as far as you're concerned, nobody did."

"Fine!" Keliegh growled before rushing back out of the morgue to his car.

Chapter 15

Shashoni barely cracked the door after Keliegh knocked relentlessly. "Go away," she whined.

"Open the door, baby. What's the matter with you?"

"I can't talk about it," she cried.

Pushing the door open, he stormed in like Bogart.

She stepped back. She was wearing a robe and her hair was a mess. Dark circles had formed under her sleepless red eyes. She looked as if she'd been through the mill.

"What's going on?"

Holding back for a moment longer she finally burst into tears, falling into his open arms. "Oh, Keliegh. I was abducted by aliens!"

"What?" he asked. Holding back his first thoughts, he held her up. He supported her in her clearly weakened state, while moving her over to her sofa. Shashoni looked frightful and although Keliegh didn't believe for a moment it was aliens, he did know something horrible had happened. Besides, where had she been since the shooting last night? Where was she *during* all that madness?

"They kidnapped me and, well . . ." She shook her head vehemently as if trying to forget. "It was awful."

Keliegh held her tight now, as she cried pitiably in his arms. His mind spun while trying to get ahead of her side of this conversation. He had nothing to say that would help, so he planned to just listen. After a moment or two, she kissed him, urging him to return the affection. Moving his hands inside her robe, he found her naked underneath. Sex for pity . . . pity for sex was what she wanted now. Keliegh knew the signs. No talking, just sex: that was Shashoni. "Shash, where were you?" He pushed himself back, closing her robe quickly.

"I don't know," she answered in a whiny voice. "This man grabbed me when I ran out of the bar. They threw me in a big car."

"He or they?"

"What?"

"You said 'he grabbed you' and then you said 'they threw you in the car,' which one was it?"

"He," she answered, sitting up now, showing irritation with Keliegh's lack of concern for her near-death experience. "He grabbed me and threw me in this big black car and they . . . there was a they in the car . . . they drove me to this awful place and wouldn't let me leave until just a few hours ago. Then they brought me home."

"So nothing happened. Well, I mean, something happened, but nothing. Can you ID them?"

Shashoni sat back on the sofa, fully cooling the space between them. "You don't even care that they could have killed me."

"Did you hear any names? Could you identify them if you saw a picture or heard them again? Did you call the police?"

"No." Shashoni stood and adjusted her robe, making sure she was fully covered and out of Keliegh's reach in case he changed his mind. "They said they were the police."

"And you believed them?"

She smacked her lips. "Well, I'm not believing you! What a foul attitude you have. I think we need to break up," she said, sounding impulsive.

Rolling his eyes, he stood. "Do you even know what happened last night?"

"Yes. I was kidnapped and my man was too busy with his

ex-partner to notice I was even gone until over twenty-four hours later."

"It hasn't been twenty-four hours, but—"

"Get outta here!" Shashoni rushed to the door and opened it. Keliegh stood his ground.

"I really want to know who threw you in the car. I just wish you could tell me something. Romia needs all the help—"

"Romia? Ugh," Shashoni gasped. "That's all those men were talking about too. Romia this and Romia that. They were saying she was a communist or something."

Shashoni ran out and was detained out of the way until conveniently everything was over. Why? Who knew what was about to happen? And why were they talking about Romia? Standing in the foyer in front of the door, Keliegh tried to put some thoughts together. "They were talking about Romia? The men who nabbed you were talking about her. Did they have accents?"

"Ugh," Shashoni gasped again, this time shoving him out the door. Suddenly Shashoni's door flew open. "Keliegh, come back. You need to hear this!"

"Shash, I—"

"The TV. Keliegh! It's about your ex-partner!"

Keliegh dashed back into the small apartment in time to hear the end of the newsflash.

"Again, she is believed to be armed and dangerous. Anyone seeing this woman is urged to call the San Francisco Police Department immediately. Do not try to apprehend this woman, as she is suspected to have single-handedly slaughtered five people on a killing spree, which started last night at approximately ten P.M. at The Spot tavern in the Palemos. This spree has resulted in the murder of the tavern's owner, Mike Brumsky . . ."

"Mike is really dead," Keliegh repeated, sitting back down on the sofa. Mike, their Mike, the bartender who over the years had become a friend to all on the force. The day's news was catching up to his brain, fact by awful fact. Sure he'd heard that Mike was dead, but reality was hitting him. "Dead! Romia?" How could Romia be a murder suspect?

Shashoni wrapped her arms around his shoulders, embracing him, consolingly nuzzling his neck. Slowly, her hands wandered over his shoulders to his chest, where she began to massage him sensually.

He grabbed her hands, pulling them over his head as he stood and spun to face her. "Look, this is serious!"

"I am serious. This all is very crazy and I'm scared, Kel. I need you to hold me," she added, outstretching her arms.

"Here is a picture of the suspect," the newscaster went on as a very unflattering photo of Romia flashed on the screen.

"God, she looks horrible," Shashoni gasped, turning her head toward the TV just as Romia's picture flashed on the screen. "Where did they find that god-awful photo? She needs to sue them. Well, I guess if she's out killing people it doesn't really matter. That's crazy, Kel . . . and to think that you thought you knew her."

Keliegh turned back to the screen with wide eyes, and then, without saying good-bye, he darted out the door. His head was whirling and his cell phone was ringing. It was Tommy.

He didn't pick up.

Chapter 16

Keliegh's trip out to The Spot was different from Romia's in that he was met with yellow tape, photographers, plenty of plastic gloves, and a grimacing uncle who was making his way through blood and gore while looking for evidence.

"So you knew about this?" Lawrence Miller asked Keliegh, who still seemed amazed at the sight he was seeing.

People gathering to get a glimpse of dead bodies was always what Keliegh hated most about scenes like this. He worked vice, but sometimes it overlapped with homicide and when it did, it was usually bad news.

"Tell me how in the hell you knew about this before it happened?"

"I didn't . . . I don't." Keliegh was fighting shock. "I want to know what you got, though. I want to know who's dead."

"How should I know, nobody seems to carry ID anymore."

Keliegh shook his head. He was thinking of Maxwell Huntington. How did he know about this? "Damn."

"So, you need to get back to finding your little ex-partner. We have some questions for her and if we find her first . . ." Lawrence said before gagging.

His partner then joined their conversation. Jim Beem was a shorter white guy with a cool, scruffy look. On some level he was probably considered a handsome man, but to Keliegh he just seemed like an odd little man. "You gonna puke? Please don't puke," Jim said before turning his attention to Keliegh. "Hey, Kel, you rubberneckin' or what?"

"No, just here to see if there really are dead bodies here this time," Keliegh said without thinking.

"As opposed to a crime scene without any . . . now what fun is that?" Jim asked. "My question here is how many killers?"

"One," Lawrence barked. "Witnesses say a woman fitting Romia's description came in to talk to"—he pointed at one of the body bags—"body number one, and when"—he pointed at the other three bags—"they came in, she turned into a ninja warrior and did a number on those three before tossing a knife into"—again he pointed at the first body bag in the row—"that guy."

"Who are these witnesses?"

"Kel, this is not your case. You need to leave. I'm not giving you an option, I'm giving you a direct order. Now get outta here."

"It's my ex-partner, guys. You have to let me—"

"No, we don't," Lawrence argued, fanning over a uniformed cop. "Arrest him."

The officer reached for cuffs.

Keliegh jumped back out of his reach. "Get the hell away from me. Look, Unk, you want Romia, this is not the way to get her."

"I know. An APB is the way to get her. Blasting her cute little deadly ninja ass over every newspaper in the city will get her . . ."

"Ooh, a cute little ninja ass," Jim teased before patting the officer on the shoulder, urging him to back off Keliegh and taking him back into the ongoing investigation. Jim then began pointing the photographers into the directions they needed to head into.

"Look, Unk," Keliegh then whispered. "I'll get you Romia if you promise me you guys will listen to her."

Lawrence took a deep breath as if regaining his composure. "Listen to what? Look, just get her to me. No promises."

Keliegh shook his head. "Can't work with that."

"Look, your ass better work with it because if you know where she is, you're gonna go down as an accomplice. To what, I don't know yet, but—"

"I don't. But I have a feeling she's gonna come to me."

Lawrence rolled his eyes. "Why? You sleeping with her?"

"No. No. I just . . ." Keliegh sighed. "We're soulmates, Unk. We're . . ." Keliegh rubbed his heart that suddenly began to ache with just the words he'd said.

"Whatever," Lawrence groaned while rolling his eyes.

"You recognize this?" Jim asked, holding up a small dirty piece of fabric brightly colored with the emblem Romia treasured—the phoenix.

Keliegh tightened his lips, knowing it was Romia's. He'd seen it in her apartment in a frame. He'd seen it on her gear. It was her symbol and represented who she was. This piece of fabric used to belong to her mother. He knew that much.

"No," he lied. "Look, I'm gonna go see my girlfriend," he lied, backing out of the conversation as best he could.

"You still seeing that Sha . . . sha . . ." Lawrence struggled.

"Shashoni, yeah, I'ma check with you all later," Keliegh said, realizing then they had had no idea that Shashoni had been involved the night before. Actually, it was clear that Jim and Lawrence had no clue about anything that had to do with the night before.

His cell phone rang. It was Tommy.

Man, she is always quick to catch a whistle.

Chapter 17

Only a crazy person would ride around on her motorcycle during broad daylight with a helmet that showed a brightly colored phoenix on it. Romia felt crazy and, frankly, too tired to care. There was no way she was going to hide out during all of this. But she wasn't just going to march into Maxwell's office and turn herself in. Something about that guy rubbed her the wrong way.

Right now she needed to figure out who the Shadow was and why he was helping her one minute and trying to kill her the next. It was obvious he had brought her motorcycle and helmet to her, because he had taken her helmet. But how did he get her bike back from the cops? She tried to remember all she could about him, but it was a waste, because he and she were always fighting in each other's presence. *Pretty hard to get acquainted,* she reasoned.

Entering Richmond city limits, she pulled into an out-of-the-way Japanese restaurant; one she knew served purely vegan cuisine. She smiled thinking about Keliegh and how impossible it was to convince him to give up meat. Pulling into the parking lot, she took off her helmet and loosed her hair from the staunch ponytail she wore. Still in her nightclothes, she thought about how easily she could be spotted, and unzipped her hoodie to reveal her wifebeater underneath. "I need to get on foot during the day," she reasoned. "I need to park my bike somewhere safe." Glancing at her watch, she saw that it had been only hours since the men were killed at the tavern. No doubt her face had been plastered all over the news. Glancing around at the few patrons, she gave second thought to her meal and opted for a Greek drive-thru she knew about. Quickly pulling herself back together, she jumped back on her bike and she headed for it.

Taking off her helmet while in the drive-thru, she ordered a falafel to go. She handed the girl her money and whizzed past the window before the girl would have had time to identify her. *Now to eat and figure out where to hide my bike,* she thought while she cruised the streets. She remembered this neighborhood well; it was the one she grew up on while in the foster home. She then remembered the church that her mother took her to. It was a Catholic church with many paintings on the ceiling and walls. She remembered her mother taking her there. Her mother would often go into the confessional and visit the priest—confessing to sins that Romia could only now imagine her mother to have. How could such a perfect woman have ever done anything wrong? *But then, who is my father?* Romia asked herself for the first time in many years.

Thinking again about the church, Romia figured that if nothing else, she would be able to eat in peace there. Taking Interstate 80 North to the exit before the Richmond-San Rafael Bridge, she jumped on the 580 until the next-to-last exit coming up then to the Chevron refinery. Heading left onto Tewksbury, she reached Santa Fe Avenue and West Richmond. That is where the rectory and church were. She was surprised she still remembered how to get there. It had been many years since she'd been there.

The church was open so she went in, slipping into a nice, comfortable-looking pew in the back to eat. She felt calm now. The walls, the paintings, the familiar all soothed her. The food was good as she basically inhaled it.

Leaning her head back, she must have appeared to be praying, although it had been years since Romia had done that.

Just then, on the ceiling she noticed the tapestry embedded in the ceiling's artwork. Cocking her head to the side, she tried to follow the design. "I don't believe it," she mumbled, noticing a familiar one. She reached inside her bra, only to find her tapestry piece missing. She began patting herself madly, pulling her clothes from her body and looking down the front of them. She must have lost it in the fight back at The Spot. She had to get back there before the police found it.

Just then, the priest entered the cathedral hall where she was. She stood quickly and quietly, hoping to leave before he engaged her in conversation. She needed to get out of there, to sort the questions that were forming in her mind based on what she had just seen—or thought she had seen. The priest saw her and jumped. "Hello, child, you startled me. I had no idea anyone was here."

"I'm not, I'm leaving. Thanks for the use of your place," she said coolly, picking up her helmet and her empty food container.

"Why are you running away? Stay and pray. You're hurt," he said, noticing the tear in Romia's sleeve. She had forgotten about it, considering she didn't bleed heavily from anywhere else except her mouth. Apparently, the cut was just a graze as it had all but healed, or so it appeared.

"Thanks, Father, but no. I mean, not today. I'm not Catholic for one, and I'm kinda in a hurry for another."

"Are you in trouble? You don't look rested. Have you been traveling?" he asked.

"Stop with the questions!" she snapped. "I'm a cop. I'm not supposed to rest. That's my job," she smarted off. He looked at her sideways as if suddenly recognizing her . . . *perhaps from the newspaper*, she thought immediately.

"You're the one they're looking for," he said.

"Look. I'm innocent. I haven't murdered anyone . . . not in the true sense of the word. I . . ." Romia stammered, watching the priest grow nervous. He wasn't like the ones on television who seemed to read minds and hearts. He was scared, and any minute would probably break and run for the phone. "Listen, Father, I'm going to leave now and you can do what you want."

"No! Don't leave. They asked me to keep you here should you realize your destiny and come here. You're . . . you're the Phoenix," he said in a foreign language that, for a second, Romia felt she understood. The chill that ran down her spine shook her whole body instantly.

"What did you just say?" she asked, thinking maybe her ears were playing tricks on her.

"You need to stay," he said, clearly in English now.

"Not gonna happen," she said before dashing out the back door of the church and hopping on her Phoenix, which she decided just that moment to name her bike. The way the bike just reappeared at that tavern was as if rising from the ashes. It was magical indeed.

Riding around for hours, the day slipped away.

"Keliegh, pick up the phone. I need to talk to you," she said into the receiver after having stopped at a pay phone. She figured it was the safest way to contact him. Waiting only a second longer, she hung up and trudged back to her bike. She rode a while longer, jumping on Highway 1 and exiting at Half Moon Bay. Stepping off the bike, she pulled the helmet off and loosened her hair, pulling the rubber band around her wrist. She noticed her torn sleeve now and examined the nick for the first time. It was a little tender, but not enough to bother her. She thought about Mike for the first time today. He was dead.

She was sure the wrong people were dying in this battle. *And I don't even know why I'm at war. But I do know I'm the one they are after . . . whoever they are. Mike shouldn'a died.* She shook her head sadly. She thought about the three men who had come to the tavern and attacked her. The accents . . . She tried again to place them but everything moved so quickly. *How did they know about . . . ?* She turned her helmet and looked at the emblem. *But then that just let me know they wanted me. They were there to get me. But why?*

Looking around, she noticed the beach was basically empty, only a couple of dog walkers. She took her helmet under her arm as she ventured down the rocky crag toward the water's edge. Looking out over the bay, she tried to sort her feelings. She'd killed today, with her bare hands. She'd done what she was sworn to never do. "But I had to," she said aloud.

She felt unlike herself. She felt as if maybe . . .

Maybe her strange dreams had come true.

"That dream. My gosh, it was so horrible," she said, re-membering it, speaking aloud. It didn't matter that she spoke at full voice. No one was noticing her, no one cared. The tall man walking his dog had no overt awareness of her presence. The lonely looking woman just walked with folded arms, star-ing out over the ocean as she meandered mindlessly along. Surely that woman wasn't noticing her. "It's as if they can't see me. It's as if I'm dead and they can't see me." It was a strange feeling—almost an invisible feeling. Romia had never felt the sensation before—as if she were dead, yet walking among the living.

Quickly, she shook her head free of the morbid thought. "Come on, chosen one," she said to herself, using the term of endearment her mother used for her when teasing. No one other than her mother had ever referred to her as such, even in jest. She felt chosen by no one other than her mother. When her mother died, she felt nothing more than the oppo-site: unchosen, unwanted, alone. "It's just not that serious," she said, contemplating her morbid thoughts and chuckling under her breath.

Turning to climb back up the rocks, she stopped suddenly

at a sight that confused and, for a second, frightened her. There at the top of the crag stood the white man from the night before.

The dead man.

He was smiling at her, the front of his shirt red with blood.

"What the . . ." she gasped. "You're not dead! Who are you?" she cried out. She rushed up the jagged hillside, back to where she had parked her bike. She was trying not to take her eyes off him for fear he would disappear, but her feet were missing solid landings. She was sliding, stumbling, fumbling.

"Wait right there!" she called out, gaining solid footing and moving quickly up the crag.

The man fanned his hand and started walking away.

"Wait!" she screamed, slamming the helmet on her head and doubling her speed up the hillside.

Reaching the top, she looked for him but only saw the dust his motorcycle kicked up, and the woman riding on the back of it. "Dammit!" She stomped. "Dammit," she spat again, before running to her motorcycle to follow them.

She gasped suddenly, noticing her jacket lying neatly over the seat. Looking around again for any sign of the man, she reached slowly for her jacket. Her hands shook. "What's happening to me?" she asked, shrugging into the leather. The comfort came immediately. She rubbed the sleeves, inhaling the scent. "Hello, old friend. I could have used you when that fool was cutting at me. Where have you been?" she asked her favorite garment. Just then, she realized again how quickly her arm had seemed to heal. A smile crept to her lips. "Well, at least I wasn't chosen to bleed to death."

Mounting her bike, she headed in the direction the man and woman had gone. Finding him was a fantasy now, she knew, but at least she could try.

Strangely enough, the panic she once felt was leaving her heart. She felt almost euphoric, otherworldly. Perhaps it was the satisfaction that indeed she hadn't killed that man. Perhaps it was insanity showing its head through her logical senses. Either way, giving up without much effort, she turned south and headed down the peninsula until she reached Santa Cruz. There she sat on the beach until sunset. She sat there, emptying her head of all rational thoughts and fears. Finally, she pulled herself together. She needed to confront Maxwell Huntington. She needed to find out who those men were who tried to kill her back at The Spot. She needed to confront her fears of being arrested and confined.

Climbing on her bike, she headed back north to the city. She was tempted to go back to the church but changed her mind. Instead, she headed where she felt she would find understanding.

She was in the middle of something—a key player maybe. Unfortunately for her, she didn't even know the game, let alone the rules.

Chapter 18

Twenty-nine years ago

The power had gone to his head. It was just that simple. Even he had to admit it. It wasn't that complicated of a situation. Focusing on natural abilities, extrasensory perceptions, and biophysical anomalies, the Phoenix had trained up a team of young people who to the outside appeared to be supernatural, paranormal, and beyond mysterious.

Phoenix played on those natural talents and the gullibility of those young people in order to build his own empire. He had governments eating out of his hand. Bidding for assignments turned eventually into those same people begging for his help. Soon it didn't matter whose side of the flag he was on, as long as the price was right.

A life of luxury he had and provided for those he'd raised as he would his own children—along with his own children. Yes, the Phoenix had children, yet he'd only claimed one: Stone.

Stone was his pride and joy.

Everyone figured it was because of his confident ways and leadership abilities, but Stix knew differently. He knew Stone's secret. He had pyrokinetic abilities. He was a fire freak—just like the Phoenix was. Once Stone got older he actually put two and two together and figured out the reason the Phoenix was the Phoenix and yes, it all had to do with this ability of his—this heightened physical anomaly that enabled him to start fires at will. Stone was young when he realized he had the ability as well. At first it scared him, but after a little training he quickly began to use it to his advantage.

"And it's not fair when you're a true leader," Stix explained. "All that hocus pocus really can only take you so far."

"So what are your abilities, considering you claim that the Phoenix is your father too?" She asked, as if knowing the answer.

"He *is* my father and, no, I have no such 'abilities.'"

"So you felt disfavored?"

"Unchosen would be more appropriate of a word, but yes. It's not as if Stone is any older. We were born on the same night," Stix continued.

"Ah, twins of a different mother. I've heard of that phenomenon as well."

"There is no hocus pocus in that. My father—our father—was just a man whore who liked his share of women and had no respect for precautions or birth control methods."

"You hate your father, don't you?" again her question seemed rhetorical.

Stix looked away from the woman and then turned back to look deep in her eyes. He wished now that he had the mental abilities of Capri, that of clairsentience, so that he could read her thoughts, or of electrokinesis so that he could show her something powerful, such as turning on and off the lights with his mind. Or maybe even if he, like his brother, had inherited the heightened senses that would allow him to start a fire from his chair.

"Maybe I just hate everyone," he admitted.

"So you no longer profess loyalties to this group, and we can have your help in tracking them down and arresting them." The female special agent asked.

"And in return I get what?"

"You get amnesty." The female agent assured.

For allowing him to hunt down his family like dogs, Stix would be able to avoid prison.

Chapter 19

An unsolved case of hit and run, that was all the report said. Unsatisfactory, as far as Romia was concerned. She'd never looked into her mother's death file this closely before but now, in light of all that was happening, she could only start there for answers. This was the library. She had gone there earlier in the day. It was a public record she pulled up, and she had to wonder how much she was really learning and how much was just made up.

Murder? Could someone have murdered her? Why?

Her mother was a private person. She loved to laugh. She enjoyed walks in the park, snuggling, and making cocoa on cold nights. They lived quietly, that Romia remembered. No grandparents, no aunts, uncles, cousins, or father. Mother was all Romia had. When she was taken from her, Romia had nothing. Fighting curbed her anger and being a cop curbed her loneliness. When the force took away her ability to fight outside the competitive ring, she was okay with it; she had Keliegh, her partner and only friend.

When he moved on in his career, she was given another partner. The void was obvious and the discomfort between her and her partner clear. But still, she had Keliegh as a friend, her only one. Eventually, with her friendship to Keliegh came Tommy, which was okay. Tommy seemed to know her need for Keliegh and never challenged or made an issue of Romia's place in Keliegh's life. Now, for no reason at all, everything was crazy. Everything was twisted around. Even

Keliegh seemed to not trust her anymore. She was about to lose it all. The anger was returning, and so was the loneliness. She wanted to fight, to bite, to hate—the same way she felt for many days, weeks, and months after her mother died.

A father? The thought of that just made her angrier.

Maybe Tommy was right, maybe she needed to just turn herself in and get this over with. All this running was making her sick and getting her nowhere closer to anything close to the truth.

Romia knew she would kill again if pressed. That, alone, was breaking her peaceful heart; the one she felt her mother had left her within the power of the phoenix tapestry, which to Romia was the symbol of peace and power over self. Her mind wandered now while sitting at her mother's gravesite. She'd been there for hours at the cemetery.

Why did that man call me Phoenix? What did he mean? How did he know about the tapestry or the meaning behind it? Did he know? Do I even know?

Tonight she would turn herself in to Maxwell Huntington. She would give up the quest for understanding. Maybe while behind bars the powers that be would get to the bottom of the mystery that shrouded her life right now. Or maybe she would just fade away into invisibility, the way she believed she was headed right now.

"How could I have seen a dead man?" she asked her mother's headstone. "Was that a symbol? No. He had my jacket." She shook her head. "I don't understand any of this."

She touched the cool concrete of the tombstone. She again thought about her mother's beauty. Her voice. Her smile. Romia felt her eyes burn but fought the tears back by sucking in a chest full of air.

"Who is my father?" she asked out of the blue. It was a question she'd never pondered before. "I need him right now," she added.

Perhaps it was Maxwell Huntington that spurred on her inquiry. He was so intimidating and forceful. She felt the need to give in to his demands. It was the way she always felt a father would make her feel: compliant. She sure would have preferred a father over Maxwell, however. She knew that even without meeting her father.

"Because I don't trust Maxwell," she told her mother's memory. "I don't trust anyone, really," she mumbled, rising to her feet. "But if you told me to trust my father, I'd find him and I'd trust him. I know you want me to trust Keliegh and I do."

Chapter 20

Reaching his apartment, Keliegh was done looking for Romia. He had no real idea of where to start. He'd watched her apartment for hours. "As if she'd be dumb enough to go back there. I know that about her. I know she wouldn't do that. I know . . ." He realized after a second longer pause that he didn't know that much about her. "How am I supposed to know who she killed without knowing anything about her?" And there was no way of knowing who was killed at The Spot besides Mike, not without having his uncle break a million rules and jeopardizing his career.

Romia's situation had his head hurting. He was too filled with pride to admit his heart hurt as well.

He wanted to talk to her. He needed to talk to her. Peeking out his window, he noticed the unmarked car. He'd given the guy a run for his money all day, following him since the moment he'd left that morning. Keliegh paced his apartment like a caged animal. He'd put in a call to Tommy and was waiting for her to get back to him.

Glancing over at his cell phone that sat on his kitchen counter, he noticed thirteen earlier missed calls. Most of the calls were from Tommy. Checking his phone for the messages, he saw that there were only three from Shashoni. He figured Tommy would not have left a voice mail. He noticed one call from an unknown number. He pondered the unknown call that had come in earlier, wondering if it was from Romia. He wondered how he'd missed that call. "Too much focus on saving her, I end up missing a chance to talk to her—shit!" he blurted, tossing his cell phone onto the sofa. He missed her.

I missed the opportunity to sleep with her . . . What a thought at a time like this, he realized, feeling his body reacting instantly to the thought of Romia under better circumstances. Her uncommon smile. Her rare laughter. The opportunity to make her his . . .

He missed that the most.

"Aw, Romia, why'd you run?" he asked aloud. His mind was too cluttered with too many thoughts.

Deciding to wash his troubles down the drain, he headed down the hall toward the bathroom. Stripping down, he stepped into the shower, sudsing up and washing down, dipping his head under the water flow, before shampooing his woolly mess. The water was hot and the bathroom steamy. "Why did you kill Mike? What's happening to you? Why did you run?" he asked. He leaned into the wall of the stall, feeling the water against his back.

"Because I had to run," Romia said then, startling him. He threw open the shower door without thinking.

"How long have you been standing there?" Keliegh asked before snatching his towel from the bar and wrapping it around himself.

"Long enough to know you doubt me," she said.

He stepped completely from the shower now. "I would never doubt you. How long have you been standing there?" It was obvious she'd been watching him shower. The glass was marbled, but she could see his body. He wondered now for a moment if perhaps tonight they would find comfort in each other's arms. But Romia said nothing. It was as if seeing him naked had not even affected her as a woman. "Why'd you come here if you think I'm not your friend?"

She looked around nervously and then back at him. "I'm tired," she admitted. "And—"

"And you're scared?" He wrapped a towel around his middle.

"No," she answered quickly.

She was lying. Keliegh could see it in her eyes, but didn't push it. She looked tired and dirty. He fanned his hand toward the running water. "You wanna? I mean, you might as well, just in case someone is listening from outside to the water running. I mean, I'm normally in there a lot longer."

"They're still out there watching you, I see, well, at least one car," Romia said, sounding serious as usual. All business, that was Romia. "They probably followed you all day. Not sure if you were gone long enough for them to bug this place but they coulda . . . Nah, they woulda been in here by now if they had bugged you," she rambled, sounding suspicious and disjointed.

"But then again, that's if they are even cops. I have to wonder, ya know." She'd stepped out to the hall suspiciously before moving back into the bathroom. She pulled off her jacket and hoodie underneath. Keliegh moved out of her way while she began to undress. He noticed her torn hoodie and the nick on her arm. "Things are coming together in my head. I was at the church and some crazy stuff ran through my head—"

"Do you need me to, um," Keliegh stammered, pointing toward the hallway, fighting his erection as she slid down the strap of her bra.

"You can turn around," she answered, still holding a straight face.

"Oh, yeah," he said, turning his back to her while she got naked. He knew she was naked because he could see her from the corner of his eye in the mirror over the sink. He tried not to watch, but he couldn't help it. She was so beautiful—her Mediterranean coloring. The way her dark hair fell between her shoulder blades nearly drove him over the edge. Her small waist and long legs . . .

Former partner or not, Romia was still a woman and he was still a man and tonight she was all woman and more. She showered quickly, sudsing up and rinsing off, copying him by dipping her head under the water flow as well. She didn't shampoo her hair, however, but simply rinsed it. He watched her through the mirror's reflection. She then shut the water off.

Thinking quickly, he grabbed his robe off the back of the door and reaching backward handed it to her.

"You can turn around now," she said before her eyes glanced downward. Finally, as if just noticing his erection tenting the towel, she blushed slightly. She quickly picked up her clothing, walking past him into the dark hallway.

Keliegh couldn't keep the embarrassment and naughty grin from flashing across his face. "Sorry about that. Hey."

She turned to him before heading into his bedroom.

"How do you get in here?" he asked, impressed again with her talents of getting in and out of his apartment unnoticed. He clicked off his bedroom light and peeked out the curtain to see who he might see staking out his place. The area looked clear and the streetlight shone through the slats of the blinds helping him to see Romia fairly easily in the room.

"I don't know. I just . . . walked in," she answered. "I've always been good at it. People see what they expect to see. They are out there waiting to see me, yet when they do, they don't. Get me? It's just too obvious for their brains to comprehend. I asked my sensei about it and he told me I had a gift for the optical illusion."

"Well, you're damn good," he admitted before turning back to her. She was sitting on his bed now, untangling her undergarments from her clothing. Again an erection formed. She didn't seem to notice this time. Keliegh couldn't control his feelings tonight, but he knew he'd have to get a grip. He had questions that needed answers. Turning from her, he pulled on his sweats, dropping the towel to the floor and adjusting himself the best way he could.

"Hey, aren't you gonna ask me how I got my helmet and jacket back?" she said, pointing to the helmet that lay on the floor by his bedroom door, showing that she'd been in his room. He could only figure she'd gotten there before him, perhaps arriving earlier that evening.

"I didn't know you didn't have it."

"Yeah, the Shadow took it," she said.

Her words sounded sincere, yet Keliegh flinched at the content of them. "Shadow?"

"Yeah, I told you last night; dude was waiting for me when I came from The Spot. He was behind the bar by my bike, we tussled, he popped my chops, and then I heard the scream. Oh, yeah, another thing, I never heard the shot. Did anyone even hear a flippin' shot?"

"Aston apparently said he did."

"He's a damn liar then," Romia cursed, catching Keliegh off guard. "Because there was no shot. There was no way that dude was shot!"

"What? Romia, now come on, I was there too, baby. I saw the body. He was shot. He was bloody."

"No." Romia fanned her hand over her belongings. "I saw him today. He gave me back my jacket. Somebody that night took my bike and my jacket and the Shadow took my helmet and, well, look, I've got it all back! So it wasn't the cops, and, oh, yeah, did anybody get my piece? Was it checked for powder? Check it for powder . . . well, on second thought, somebody's probably fired it by now, considering all this is just a damn setup." She cursed on, sounding less and less like the Romia he knew. "If my piece even makes it to evidence."

Keliegh was worried now. Was Romia really losing it? Could she be as crazy as they said? When she fled the night before, she had on her jacket and her helmet, and was on her bike.

When had she lost those things and regained them? And of course her gun was in evidence. Maxwell Huntington had it that night during the interrogation. "Romia, when's the last time you slept?"

"I got in about three hours at Tommy's."

"Your place is trashed. Did you do that?"

"Why would I do that? When would I do that?" she asked.

"Dunno. Maybe you were looking for something."

Her eyes were wide. He could see that, even in the dimly lit room.

"Why would I trash my place looking for something?" Romia asked. "Them jokers that followed me to The Spot musta done it. You are not listening. I said I saw the guy everybody thinks I shot. I'm debating meeting with the IA guy. I mean, this is big." She spoke excitedly, although in a quiet voice. "Keliegh, it was those dudes at The Spot. They killed Mike and I killed them for killing Mike. They had accents."

Keliegh put caution to the wind now and walked over to where Romia was sitting. He put his hands on her shoulders firmly. "Romia, baby, you're not making sense. You're in trouble and I wanna help you, but you gotta make sense."

She pushed his hands off as if dusting her shoulders. "Listen to me, I know what I saw! Today I saw him and that chick who was screaming. He had blood on his shirt and she had on the same dress and everything. I tried to get up the hill to talk to him but I couldn't catch them because they split on a bike. I think it was a Harley but . . ." She sounded manic now. "But he left my jacket and check this out. I went to the church to eat and guess what I saw on the ceiling." She began looking through her clothing for the tapestry. Thats right, it was gone. "I can't find it, but it was on the ceiling of the church. Why would there be pictures of a phoenix on the ceiling of a church, for goodness sake. It must mean something. I mean, I was drawn there and I remember my mother taking me there as a child and it must mean something." She rambled on, still looking for the tapestry, not accepting that she'd lost it.

Keliegh squatted down in front of her. He wanted to hold her. He knew she needed to be held but he didn't dare. He just rested his hands on her bare thighs, wanting to explore higher. He wanted to be inside her right now. Not for the orgasm, but for the peace. He wanted to give her peace and calm. She needed it.

"Something weird is happening to me . . ."

Just then, his cell phone rang. He looked in the direction of the phone and then back at her. She nodded. He stood and left the room to answer it.

"What's up?" he asked.

It was Tommy. "Don't know where to start."

"Start? Start at the start."

"To start, Romia killed a buncha people today!"

"Yeah," Keliegh said in nearly a whisper.

"Yeah, that and uh . . . you're not suspended."

"What the hell?"

"That's what I said. Just heard Captain ranting and raving around here about you not calling in. "

"That's bull. I'm calling the captain myself. They told me I was suspended."

"They who?"

"That Maxwell cat, I told you that! Better yet, I'm on my way in," Keliegh said, reaching for a shirt that hung on the back of a dinette chair. "I'ma bring—"

"No, now wait; you say this cat, Maxwell What's-His-Name told you that you were suspended?"

"Yeah."

"Well, nobody knows who that *cat* is. IA is headed up by some dude named Roberson. I checked that, too."

"Okay, but what about the shooting last night at The Spot? Where is the body?"

"Nobody seems to know about that, either."

"What about Hank and Aston?"

"I never did see Aston. Aston never did show up and now, poof, can't get my hands on Hank either. No reports. Nothing happened, and I can't find Aston or Hank to confirm anything."

"Okay, so you're trying to tell me that this is some big hoax or gag? What about today? Mike . . . I just went out there to The Spot. Mike's dead!"

"Oh, he's dead all right. I got that verified for sure. Now that news is all over the joint—with Romia's name in the same sentence."

"Yeah, but Rome said—"

"You've spoken to her?"

By then Keliegh had walked back into his bedroom to let Romia know he was talking to Tommy and that they were both prepared to help her. But she was gone. There wasn't a trace of her. There was just an opened window. "Shit!" He stomped his foot in frustration looking around, under the bed, in the closet. "No," Keliegh lied, sounding instantly deflated.

"Where is she, Keli?"

"She didn't do it," was all he could say.

"She was in my place last night," Tommy said.

"Yeah, so?"

"So! I went home and guess what? My place was trashed, tossed, and otherwise destroyed."

"What were they looking for?"

"Who is they? It was her. She's nuts, Kel. Maybe she was just pissed at me for interrupting your little shower thing. Just like she killed Mike for giving her the wrong drink. I heard about it . . ."

"Come on, Tommy, she's not shallow like that and there was no shower thing. Besides, her place was trashed too."

"Maybe she trashed her own place and then mine. The

cushions were ripped to shreds as if someone took a knife to them. It was like a crazy maniac jealous bitch took a knife to them. Look, she could really be nuts."

"Are you on a drug? What the hell is wrong with you? I never knew you hated her so much."

"I don't hate her, but look, you could be in danger. You're my partner, and I don't care if it was your mother—nobody is gonna . . ." Tommy seemed to catch her words. "I'm getting in this thing. If nothing else to keep you safe, whether I like it or not."

"I'm sorry, Tommy, I'm sorry about all this," Keliegh said, rubbing his head. "But I can't have—"

"Sorry? No. Don't 'sorry' me out of this. I know what you're about to say, but no."

"Fine! But if you're going to 'help' you have to believe she's innocent!"

"No, I don't. I have to believe in what's right and pursue that. If she falls on the wrong side of it then there ya go. But for now, nothing seems right and I can't work with that."

Just then he heard a noise coming from outside his condominium. It was the sound of an engine shutting off. The unmarked car had just returned from somewhere. *What kind of surveillance is that? What'd he do, leave for donuts?* "Hang on, Tommy," he blurted, tossing the phone on the couch and marching out of his house toward the parked car. The man inside looked at him as if suddenly nervous. Keliegh had never seen him before. He wasn't from his own precinct, nor did he look like anyone he'd seen at his uncle's precinct.

Keliegh grabbed at the locked door. "Open the door! Open it, you mother!"

"What? What?" the man asked, lowering the window slightly. Keliegh could hear Top Forty music coming from his radio. He was nowhere near set up for police surveillance.

"Who are you? Why are you watching my place?"

"I'm a security guard. I work at the mall. I took this gig for some moonlighting money."

"What? Who hired you?"

"Some dude. I don't know his name," he explained.

"Big black guy?" Keliegh asked, jerking at the door again.

"Maybe . . . maybe," the guy answered, holding tight to his side of the door. "He told me to watch your place and then he'd check in with me periodically to get a report. He told me to leave when you leave and follow you around. So I did. But I took a little, you know, break. Had to go . . . you know. Too much coffee, I guess," the guy explained.

Keliegh slammed his hand on the window forcefully. "Get outta the car!"

"What? Hell no."

"I said, get outta the car!" Keliegh barked.

Instead of obeying, the guy started the car and peeled off, causing Keliegh to spin off the car and stumble a little bit. Catching his balance, Keliegh stomped and spit. "Shit!"

Storming back into his place, he knew he had to call Tommy back now. He'd screwed up. There was no doubt. He'd let Romia get away and it was more than clear now that nothing was what it was appearing to be.

Stepping inside and slamming the door behind him, he glanced over at his sofa, noticing the shadowy figure sitting there. The man reminded him quickly of the pictures he'd seen of ninjas. Surely this wasn't a true ninja. *Was it?* With all the other crazy shit going on, he could only hope not. Keliegh immediately took assessment of his mind and his weapon . . . neither was where he wanted them to be. Suddenly, he remembered Romia's description of the man who attacked her behind the tavern.

"You're the Shadow?"

"Nice name. You make that up?" the man asked, jumping to his feet and taking a fighting stance. Keliegh was a sharp shooter, not a fighter. This wasn't gonna be pretty, he could tell.

"You are so going to kick my ass, huh?" Keliegh asked.

The Shadow chuckled wickedly.

Chapter 21

Tommy loudly explained that she was leaving to follow a lead she had on a case she was working. She'd been talking in a low volume to Keliegh, hoping nobody had been paying attention, because she didn't want them to know what she and Keliegh were up to. They were flying solo on this case and not sure what side they were fighting for: Romia's or the law.

"Turner, meeting, let's go!" The captain snapped his fingers as he stepped from the glass elevator that brought him down from the second-floor perch. Everyone hated this new addition to their building. If the captain didn't feel as though he was a demigod before he sure did now, with the way he could look out over the low sides of the balcony above. He would watch without anyone really noticing until it was usually too late. The captain pointed toward muster room three.

"But I was . . ." Tommy sighed, realizing she was talking to the back of his head as the short man headed down the hall.

In the meeting room

"Okay, everyone, listen up. I know this is really a tough one, but it has to be done. We got a swerve on our hands and so our duty as officers of the law is to pick her up and bring her in. No heroics, and by the book," the captain said, aiming his comment toward Aston. Tommy realized then he was present.

"At this point, we've had IA dentify the folks killed at The Spot and, unfortunately, they were not from our neighborhood. They were dignitaries from the government of a friendly country just out for a stroll," the captain went on. Everyone groaned as if realizing the political implications.

"So, folks, this case is no longer entirely in our hands. IA is working with foreign secret service to get this thing taken care of before it escalates to . . ." the captain looked around as if searching for a word to represent how bad this could get. "Whatever," he said instead. "So for them to play their political games, and since officer Romia Smith is one of our own, we've been asked to bring her in for them. Now, with that said, it is not gonna be easy. She's on the fly and—"

"Cap'n, you sound like we're lookin' for Supergirl," Aston interjected, bringing laughter from a few others in the room.

"Yeah, I just think we need to put a flame on the end of that broom of hers and that'll end that 'flying' business," another one said.

"Yeah, maybe we just need to put up some posters saying there's a leather sale at Frederick's of Hollywood and that'll get her attention," another officer taunted.

Instantly, Tommy realized how her fellow male detectives felt about Romia's sexy looks. *And so what?* she thought in response to the jeering. *Romia is a good cop but all they see is a woman under that protective leather.* Tommy thought about Romia's looks: *Black leather, high heels, motorcycle. Yeah, they see a slut with a badge.*

One of the males jeering Romia turned his attention to her. As a detective, Tommy tried to dress comfortably yet ready for action. She enjoyed wearing her fair amount of leather, but she was more of a tomboy in brown suede. Not Romia. Romia was exotic. They were jealous of what they couldn't have, Tommy knew this.

What one of those guys might do if they found Romia suddenly made Tommy's flesh crawl.

Romia didn't deserve the nasty-sounding comments coming from these men. "I'll bring her in," Tommy volunteered, speaking above the snide remarks.

"No, Turner. Your partner is all wrapped up in this . . . way too close for my comfort." The captain looked around. "We got asked to help, we said okay. If we see her we'll nab her. If we don't, then *c'est la vie*."

"I can bring her in. Nobody else is gonna be able to," Tommy continued to push.

"Oh? Since when can you take her?" Aston blurted.

"Why does everyone think she needs a fight? Has anyone even considered that she might be innocent? Besides, why are you even here? Why didn't you get suspended like Keliegh?"

"Maybe because I didn't do anything wrong. Unlike Keliegh."

"He didn't do anything but keep you from getting your ass kicked . . . again."

"Oh, yeah?" Aston jumped to his feet and so did Tommy. She knew Aston was studying martial arts, but still she could take him. He was big and bulky. Tommy's skills didn't match Romia's, but she could take Aston with no problem.

"Okay . . . okay! Let it go, folks," the captain interjected. "What suspension? I didn't suspend anybody."

"IA suspended Jack because he was obstructing. We had her, Cap'n, and Jack let her go—"

"You had nothing! Captain, has anyone thought to just talk to her and ask her what happened?" Tommy asked.

"No," a few people said in answer to what was meant to be a rhetorical question. Tommy sighed.

Even Keliegh seemed to be losing hope in Romia coming around, Tommy could tell by their last conversation. Sure, she never really had faith that Romia was innocent, but even with that, everyone deserved a chance. Even Tommy realized that Romia deserved a chance to explain the possibilities of her being innocent. Whoever was looking for her was vicious. By the looks of her own apartment she could tell that. If Romia wasn't crazy, she was in danger. And if this was how the foreign IA worked, they had some strange policies on search procedures.

Maybe she needed to visit this Mr. Maxwell guy. He seemed to be the only real lead any of them had toward getting to the bottom of all this.

Just then, a high level–looking suit walked in the room. He smelled like a fed but there was no way of knowing. He motioned for the captain to follow him. Tommy's neck stretched as far as it could before Aston's voice brought her back.

"Broads . . ." was all Tommy caught of his comment.

"What did you say?" Tommy asked him.

The room broke into challenging woof calls. She looked around for Canasta, the only other female in the precinct, and of course she was missing from this meeting. "I was sayin' that you broads always stick together!" Aston accused.

"Broads!" Tommy asked, slamming her hands on her hips, which brought on even more woof calls. "You wanna take this outside? I'll show you some stickin'. I'll stick this boot up your ass."

"Right," Aston guffawed, shaking his head in disbelief.

"I'd take the challenge, Aston. I'd love to get in a headlock with you, Tommy ol' girl," another male officer yelled out.

"Shut up, asshole," Tommy snapped, pointing her finger at him, but turning her attention back to Aston who still thought the situation was funny. Tommy stepped up to him. They both took a fighting stance. Tommy had had it up to her eyebrows and was prepared to dance Aston all around that room.

About then, the captain walked back into the room. "Whoa! You two, back away from each other! Now!" he yelled before wiping his brow. "Announcement. We're off the Smith case—completely." He stretched out his arms as if calling an out in baseball. He was perhaps calling time out for Aston and Tommy as well.

"What? Did somebody find her?" Tommy asked.

The captain's glare showed though the stare. He was pondering how much to tell her, that was clear. Or, maybe he was pondering her suspension. Who knew? "It's out of our hands, Turner. Let it go. Okay, everyone. To the streets. We all have something to do that's more important than this, and now that we've wasted a lot of time, we have less to do it in," he instructed before heading out of the office.

"Wow, we got all worked up for nothing," Aston said, following his words with a sarcastic-sounding heavy sigh, holding out his hand to shake Tommy's. "Truce?"

Tommy looked at the hand like it was rotted meat. "Screw you, Aston," she said, before storming out of the meeting room to stop the captain before he hit the elevator that would take him up to his office on the second floor. He never took the stairs, despite his weight issues.

"Cap'n, you have to tell me what's up with the Smith case. Did they find her? Tell me somethin'."

"Why?"

"Cap'n, come on now, you can't just leave me hanging like this. You know I need to know."

"Sure I can. And you don't need to know nutt'n," he stated bluntly before walking into the open elevator. "I need to know, however, where your partner is, and I also need to know why I shouldn't suspend him right now," the captain added before the door closed. Seconds later, Tommy watched him walking above her head into his office and slamming the door.

Tommy looked around, noticing a few Nosey Roseys watching her. Bob Hetchum was one in particular. He stared so hard that Tommy was drawn to his desk.

"Wow, Cap'n had some serious issues after that suit stopped in this morning. Where were you, by the way?" she asked, noticing that he and his partner were missing from the morning meeting.

Hetchum looked around and then back at her. "When Big Brother speaks, somebody gotta listen," he said under his breath.

"Big Brother?"

"Yeah, that suit was CIA."

"You shitz'n me?" she asked, trying to hide her immediate shock.

"Yeah, apparently Smith is in deep on all four corners. First the feds, now the CIA—and who knows who's next thanks to that nice little massacre out there at the bar."

"So what do you know about all this? I'm still kinda in the dark," Tommy admitted.

"Well, not much, but my sources tell me that those foreign guys were terrorists."

"What?" Tommy blurted.

Bob shushed her. "Seriously, I'm hearing they were here on"—he made quotation marks around the next word—"business that involved Romia. Seems like our little stone princess isn't who she seems to be. I mean, phone records, letters, all kinds of shit was found at her place. She's into all kinds of international stuff," he exposed. "Sounds wild, I know, but hey, with a swerve, I mean, anything could be going on. I hear her mother was communist."

"And if she was, what does that have to do with Romia?"

"I know. It's turning into a witch hunt."

"And as I always say about witches, if she is one, I wouldn't be trying to find out. Okay?" Tommy slid onto the edge of

Bob Hetchem's desk. She watched his eyes cover her thigh and then make their way up to her face. She thought about what her fellow male officers thought about Romia's sexy ways. Did they think that about her too? She slid back off the desk and stood tall with her hands in her pockets, trying to look manly as possible. "But then, with a swerve, you're right. I mean, they could be into anything and everything."

"Hey, by the way, how is Keliegh doing? I mean, he's got to be wiggin' out, Romia trying to kill him and all."

"Kill him? She didn't . . ." Tommy caught her words. She'd get more information from playing along than resisting. "Yeah, well, I'm sure he's having it rough. I mean, between him getting suspended and . . ." Tommy was playing along here. She knew Keliegh hadn't been suspended but she wanted to play dumb. She wanted to see what Hetchem would tell her.

"Suspended?" Hetchem gasped. "Where'd you hear that?"

"Same place you heard Romia was tryin' to kill him, probably? I'm guessin' the head of IA."

Hetchem's eyes widened. "Head of IA?"

"Yeah, Maxwell somebody," Tommy continued to play along. "I was gonna give him a call and . . ."

"Nobody in IA named Maxwell," Bob said, clicking away at his computer instantly. He was a bit of geek. Tommy suspected that he liked her a little bit. He had gone quickly to the data bank to pull up some information on Maxwell, no doubt.

"Really?"

"Yeah, head of IA is a guy named Roberson," he confirmed. "And, besides, why would IA have information that would help you? Why would you call them when they haven't called us?"

"Really? Nobody from IA has been down here? Wouldn't you think they would with Romia being a cop and all?"

"That suit who just left here is the first and only suit to come since this whole mess started."

"Wow," Tommy said, sounding truly impressed. She was, actually. This was the best gossip she'd had so far. "Well, I gotta try something. I mean, Keliegh is my partner."

Hetchem looked around suspiciously. "Look, Tom, you need to stay outta this web. The spider's got a lotta legs and, well, I'd hate to see you get stung. I hear things. I heard things," he said. "This is the first suit that came, but not the first like"— he made quotation marks in the air—"official type who came here."

"Who was the other guy?"

"Can't tell you."

"Tell me."

"Don't know who he was. I asked Aston, since it seems like they were chums, ya know, but I got nothin' but a hearty 'stay out of it.' So I'm telling you the same thing."

"And I hear you," she responded. He smirked at her. "No, seriously, Bob, I hear you," she assured. "Did you happen to hear the name Huntington?" she asked. About then, Aston came into earshot of their conversation. Moving over to her desk, Tommy pulled out her cell phone and called Keliegh again; he didn't answer. Pushing the red button instead of leaving a voice mail, she noticed a call come in from blocked number.

"Turner," she answered.

"Huntington."

"Really? Funny you should call me. I was just thinking about calling you," she said teasingly.

He chuckled. "That would be rather difficult, don't you think? I mean, considering I don't exist."

"Exactly, I was gonna use my 'special directory,'" she said, looking around now as if to see which wall had ears. It was clear to her that he had somehow heard her conversation with

Bob. Tommy felt instantly a little freaked out, but she tried not to let it show in her voice. It wasn't as if she hadn't been seeing and hearing some pretty strange stuff since last night. "So, tell me, my man, what's really going on?" she asked, sounding like Keliegh in one of his more cocky moods.

"You really wanna know?"

"Yeah, I really wanna know. I really do. My partner is involved, so yeah. Lay it on me."

He laughed. "You're funny. Tell you what. Why not meet me at Romia's place?"

"Romia's, why?"

"Well, I'm already here, so why not?" he answered.

"Romia with you?"

"Of course."

"Yeah, right. You sound so convincing. Mind if I tell Keliegh where we're meeting in case I disappear after talking to you? Seems like that's what happens to people who have dealings with you."

"They always come back. Look at Aston, he came back."

Looking at Aston, she tried to see if maybe he was different somehow, but with Aston who could know? "Yeah, but I bet half his brain is gone. But then again, that is his natural state, I think."

Maxwell laughed. "Well, you call your Keliegh, and tell him whatever you want. Hey, you can even call the cops if you want," Maxwell said with an evil sneer in his voice. Tommy hung up and called Keliegh again; there was no answer.

Glancing over at Bob Hetchem, she started to inform him of where she was going, but after noticing Aston heading toward him, she went with her gut on this one. It was convincing her that she and Keliegh needed to handle this without a lot of other people involved.

Maybe we'll get to the bottom of this without a lot of smoke and mirrors if we just do it his way, she thought regarding Maxwell Huntington.

Chapter 22

The Phoenix

Stone was his name, which he lived up to every day of his life. He was young, cocky, cool, and aloof, with no regard for life. He was the favored of all the Phoenix's underlings and trusted with many secrets. Stone had little respect for standards set by society and followed out orders given by the Phoenix without question. Thus, he was just this side of educated madness.

Stone led the team of young assassins and killed without flinching. He had but one weakness, a young French girl named Capri.

Against the rules, he and Capri became lovers. This decadence led to his demise. He broke the rules to save Capri's life. This led to him taking a bullet.

It didn't matter whose bullet finished him off, in Stix's opinion. With the command given, Stix took the lead, ushering Capri and Malik to safety. Stix was the leader now and, in his heart, he felt he should be recognized as such.

Upon their return to the Phoenix's lair, Stix, hoping to find understanding and perhaps even an ounce of commendation for at least saving Capri and Malik, found only a harsh rebuking.

"Stone ordered us to leave," Stix told the Phoenix. "He was dying."

"Is this true, Malik?" the Phoenix asked.

"I . . . I," Malik stumbled.

"He told us to leave," Stix explained again, wondering why his comrades were hesitating.

"We didn't want to leave. I didn't want to leave," Capri cried.

"Nor I. Stone insisted," Malik said now.

"It is the rules! There was no hesitation. He ordered us to leave," Stix continued. "He was dying!"

"And you left!" the Phoenix raged.

"Yes. We left. It was a command," Stix pleaded. "He was gut shot. He was going to die. He had lost much blood. So I—"

"You left my son to die!"

Malik and Capri looked at each other as if hearing the words for the first time. Many of them had assumed the connection between Stone and the Phoenix, but rarely did they hear it said and so plainly acknowledged.

"Yes, Phoenix. We left him to die!" Stix screamed now. His emotions were high as he was filled with confusing and growing rage.

"You now think this puts you in his place. You will never fill his place. He was my son!"

"We are all your sons," Stix barked. He was being insubordinate, but no longer cared.

The Phoenix's blue eyes blazed like diamonds. He swung on Stix, catching the side of his face in a steel blow. Stix grabbed at the pain. "You are not my son."

Suddenly, the Phoenix bayed loudly, tearing at his clothing. "You left my son to die!"

Capri turned away, unable to watch the man grieve.

"I hope it helps to know he started fire after we left. He made sure all the evidence was gone," Malik said in a low voice.

At that, the Phoenix's outcries ceased abruptly. "A fire?"

"Yes," Malik said, before breaking down in tears.

Chapter 23

Romia drove to the city, ending up back at the church. She was drawn there. She was tired and wanted to rest, if just for a moment. Maybe there her mother would answer her. Maybe through the paintings her mother would speak to her. The paintings in this place soothed her. They made her feel close to her mother again. The haunting pictures of the elusive bird seemed oddly out of place against the biblical symbols yet, then again, so apropos for her feelings right now.

Parking her bike around the back, she climbed off and quickly tiptoed up to the back door. Trying the knob, she found it locked. "You act like churches are twenty-four-hour drive-thrus," she fussed at herself before covering her fist with her jacket sleeve. With one quick punch she took out the stained glass window inlay. Surprisingly enough there was no alarm set . . . at least, not one she heard. Within seconds she was inside the darkened church. Feeling her way, she made it to a pew. "I'm not sure why I'm here, but here goes," she whispered before dropping to her knees as if to pray. "I'm not even sure where to begin," she whispered again.

Just then her cell phone rang. "What" she answered. She'd turned off all GPS signals and so had to wonder who was calling her. Who had found her?

"Maxwell."

"How come I'm not surprised?"

"You should be."

"And why is that?"

"Because you killed someone who didn't die, someone is dead who you didn't kill, and you've actually escaped three people who were trying to kill you."

"And I'm being blamed for all of it. You got a reason for that?"

"Of course."

Just then the light came on in the church. "You're really easy to follow. You're going to have to work on that," Maxwell said, closing his cell phone.

Romia was on her feet and ready to take him on, but was stopped by a quick blow to the back of the head. She was stunned but not stopped. She was quickly engaged. It was none other than her nemesis, the Shadow.

"Do you ever get enough?" she growled.

He chuckled from under the dark cover. Apparently, he'd been in the church the entire time. This opponent was driving her mad and she would never see peace until she'd destroyed him, of this she was certain. She leapt onto the pew and then in a flying leap attacked, tackling him as if on a football field. She knew he was not prepared for such a physical encounter—and she was right. Jumping on him, she slugged his face as if on a playground until finally she grabbed at the stocking mask, pulling it roughly from his head. His hair was slicked back and his green eyes were big and wild looking. "Get off me," he yelped.

Stunned at finally hearing his full voice, she was again removed from her situation by Maxwell's hard hand on her jacket, pulling her off of him.

"You two have to stop this," he said, sounding as if speaking to children.

Chapter 24

Tommy left another message on Keliegh's phone before pulling into Romia's parking lot and rushing up the flight of stairs to her place. Reaching the door, she found it ajar. Pushing it open with her foot, she drew her weapon. "Romia?" Tommy called out softly. "It's Tommy." Tommy wished Romia had answered. She wanted to talk to her. Keliegh was too close to this case. He was too emotionally involved. That was clear. Tommy just knew if she could crack this case, at least this part of it—finding Romia and finding out who this Maxwell cat was—she'd have a leg up in proving Romia's innocence.

Sure, in the back of her mind she wanted to believe Romia was innocent. It was obvious Keliegh was in love with her. She knew it from the start. Heaven knows she'd thrown herself at him enough to realize he had someone else in his heart. Okay, so there were the bimbos like Shashoni and all the others, but Tommy had long ago put those chicks in perspective. They were just something to do. Keliegh loved somebody. That was obvious by his inability to commit to any of those other women. He loved somebody he couldn't have. And Tommy knew that wasn't her. Keliegh could have her in a heartbeat!

He loved Romia.

It was getting more and more apparent that Romia was being set up, and harder to believe she was just a good cop gone bad. Maxwell had convinced her of that. Maxwell had convinced Tommy that something bigger than all of them was going on. It was one of those things that was so big that nobody could see it—like a white elephant.

Looking around the living room, it was obvious that this mess wasn't in the "oh, I'm late for work" category. Looking around, she saw that Romia's place had been trashed in a similar way to hers. Tommy figured it was done by professionals, and probably the same ones who had tossed her place. "Romia, what is everybody looking for? What did you get yourself involved in?"

Stepping lightly over the turned over coffee table, which spilled out Romia's photo album, something caught her eye. Bending down, Tommy pulled out a photo of a woman holding a beautiful baby girl. On the woman's arm, Tommy noticed a tattoo. It was the same design that Romia wore on her jacket and helmet, and that was painted on her bike in bright colors. "A phoenix?" Tommy mumbled before creeping into Romia's kitchen. Tommy opened the refrigerator door out of reflex—not sure what she'd find in there—hoping not to find anything that didn't belong in there. She closed the door, only to jump in a start at the sudden appearance of a stranger in a black body suit.

"So you made it," she whispered.

"Of course, I'm never late for a party," Tommy said, drawing her gun on her.

"Wonder who tossed this place?" she asked, sounding to Tommy as if she knew.

"We didn't," Tommy answered. "Who are you?"

"I'm a spy," she answered.

"You CIA?"

"CIA?" The woman laughed before returning to a whispered voice. "Do I look like CIA?" she asked.

"Wouldn't know," Tommy answered, getting antsy. She hated these kinds of intimidation tactics. She was one who liked to get to the point.

"Well, I'm not. I'm actually a friend, believe it or not."

"Not," Tommy said, releasing the safety, testing the woman's nerves. She didn't even flinch.

"Fair enough." The woman snatched the gun, tossing it aside. Her speed was amazing. Tommy had to admit that she only knew one other person that fast.

"Okay," Tommy said, realizing the battle before it officially started. She swung on the woman.

"Is that the best you got, Tommy? I guess it's true . . . you'll never beat me."

Tommy, for a second, let her guard waver. "Romia?"

"How did you guess?" she asked, sounding like Romia.

Tommy was unsure about this woman's true identity, but there was no time to play guessing games. The woman, with fists of fury, came at her. Tommy blocked the quick-coming punches, backing away suddenly as the shadowy figure dressed all in black, claiming to be Romia, egged Tommy back into combat.

Taking a moment to think, Tommy tested the woman. She needed to know for sure. "If you're Romia, tell me something only Romia and I would know."

"Keliegh's dick is thirteen inches long when it's hard. Oops, but then again, you don't know that do you?" the woman said, slapping Tommy quickly across the face. It was more of a taunt, but Tommy was livid and kicked high, aiming it to land with a hardy blow, but the woman blocked, catching Tommy's foot and twisting. Tommy heard the crack before she felt the pain.

The woman then without mercy worked her over.

"This is Tommy, I've got Romia. Yeah, I'm outside her place. I'm going in," the woman said to dispatch, sounding now like Tommy on the phone. "Of course it's her. Send some backup. Oh, and check on Keliegh, too. I haven't been able to reach him, and I'm afraid she's done something to him. I lost track of her partner when they split up . . . and I think he went after Keliegh."

The woman hung up Tommy's phone, dropping it next to her unconscious body. "You'll never see Romia again," the woman said. "She's one of us now. We're taking her home where she belongs."

Chapter 25

Romia stared at the picture of her mother. "How did you get this?" she asked, staving off emotions. Her mother's long, sandy blond tresses appeared to blow in the wind. Her face, soft and cherub-like, seemed poised to be photographed, although it was clear that the picture was candid. Her mother appeared ageless in the photo. There was no way for Romia to tell when it was taken. She stared then at the photo to get an idea from the background scene.

It was hard to focus, considering all things around her. The church setting was the one place where serenity should have reigned, yet it was overtly absent.

The picture was snatched from her hands by the tall dark man she had come to know as Maxwell Huntington, although she now doubted his true identity. He handed her another picture. This one was of a handsome man who looked around forty-something. "Who is this?" she asked.

Maxwell snatched the photo back and slid it back into a file. Again and again he showed her several pictures of people she didn't know.

"Who are they? What do they have to do with me? How did you get a picture of my mother?" she asked. He then handed her another photo of a woman around her age. She looked like her mother, but was far too old to be her. Her mother had died as a much younger woman. She had dark hair and eyes that didn't look like her mother's, yet . . .

Maybe the woman was a relative, for she had an oddly tell-

ing face that moved Romia to stroke the picture in an unconscious gesture, or perhaps to beg for a connection.

"Do you know her?" Maxwell asked again.

Romia hesitated again and then looked up at Maxwell.
"No," Romia answered truthfully. Slowly, he took the photo
from her this time. No gruffness. He then handed her the
photo again of the middle-aged man. He was handsome, but
surely she didn't know him. "You know him?"

"No," Romia sighed, suddenly tired of this interrogation.
"I told you that!" she spat. It was getting them nowhere closer
to why she was here and why she had been made a victim
of this charade. Why was she being held here at this church
against her will? She had come to pray, not be held captive.
"Do you know them? Answer me for a change! You're not the
only one who wants answers, Mr."—she paused before saying
his name—"Huntington."

He smiled. "Interesting."

"Not to me. But finding out why you have a photo of my
mother is very interesting to me. She was never in trouble
with the police before she died. Why was she being spied on?"

"You were a baby when she was murdered, what do you
know about her?"

Romia snapped, "She wasn't murdered." She jumped to
her feet, only to be slammed back into her seat by the woolly
headed young man.

He had catlike reflexes that were, somehow, familiar to
Romia. His hair had been loosed from the tight ponytail he
wore and was wild on his head. He caught Romia's attention
suddenly. She stared at him for a second. His skin was olive
in tone, his eyes, green—dazzling green. She'd seen eyes like
his before. She looked at his hands, long and slender. Yes,
she had met this man before, or someone like him. But his
crooked smile instantly brought her back from the reverie.

Immediately, she wanted to take him on again. She wanted to fight him.

"Shadow," she mumbled as if it were a bad word. She then noticed the wicked smirk creep to his face.

The man she supposedly had shot the night before had joined him not too long into this interrogation session. Not too long afterward, the woman entered the room. She, too, was familiar. Romia pictured her with blond hair instead of her natural dark color. "It's you!" Romia accused. The woman ignored her exclamation. She was the woman who had framed her at the tavern. Who were these people?

"It's done. Tommy is out. She won't be looking for this one anytime soon," the woman said before adding something in another language.

"What?" Romia blurted. "Out? What has happened to Tommy?"

"And Jack as well?" Maxwell asked the man, ignoring her. The man nodded. "They were going to be too much trouble for us anyway. So we can proceed before any other obstacles get in our way," Maxwell added.

The tiny hairs were up on the back of Romia's neck and she was on total alert. The people in this room were an odd group. In Romia's mind, they resembled circus people or gypsies. But none of that mattered now. They had done something to Tommy and Keliegh, so that made them the enemy.

"Have you checked the airports?"

"Yes, there were no red flags. I think he thought those goons won." Everyone laughed with that comment.

"They don't know who they're fooling with. Those goons were kid's play. Now we are all together and we shall get this finished," Maxwell said, putting the pictures back in the envelope.

"Who are you people?" Romia blurted out, trying to gather

some sense from what seemed to be a casual conversation about her going on around her.

"I guess you know I'm not really IA," Maxwell confessed, standing and pacing slowly around the room. It seemed as though at first they were readying to leave, but he appeared to have something to get off his chest.

"Nah, just sorta fell for that one," Romia sneered sarcastically. In her mind, she was looking for a moment. She just needed one moment to act. "But fool me once, shame on you."

Maxwell smiled slyly, turning back to her. "And you . . . you're not who you think you are either."

"Now there you're wrong. I'm Romia Smith. I'm a cop. And as soon as I get out from under this"—she looked around, regarding the church's basement—"chamber of horrors, I'm gonna arrest you. All of you."

Suddenly the room broke into laughter. Now the people engaged in a conversation that no longer was spoken in English.

Romia looked around at everyone: the "dead man" from The Spot, the one who she supposedly shot with her police revolver; the blond woman who suddenly appeared in the darkness, screaming bloody murder for all to hear and framing her as the killer; the Shadow, who matched her talent in martial arts and bloodied her lip to make it appear as though she had tangled with the undead man before shooting him; and Maxwell Huntington, the IA officer who, as Mike said, "cleaned that place up as if nothing had happened." They were all there, laughing at her. The only missing members of this party were the three men who attacked her. Maybe they would soon show up to finish the job. Maybe they too would be undead and here to make this macabre theater act complete.

At that point, Romia leapt to her feet again. The Shadow

was on her, but he had been too distracted jeering her, so she got in three rotating punches and a kick before he could block. The last sent him into the nearest wall. Maxwell stepped forward but Romia attacked first, with a spin kick that caught his chin, stunning him momentarily.

The woman pulled a gun, but Romia caught the barrel, snatching it from her hand and dismantling it instantly. She raised her fist and, without looking, slammed the back of her fist against the undead man's face, turning then and headbutting him. The woman kicked her feet from under her, yet when Romia hit the floor, she grabbed the empty weapon only to slap the attacking woman with it.

The Shadow, only stunned, kicked her in the ribs while she was down. She could see now that this time he was holding back nothing. This blow was much harder than their encounter in the dark upper room, when he had taken her helmet. This time they were not sparring. This was now a full-on battle, one she had prepared for her whole life. Rage consumed her as she let go of a barrage of movements she was certain he had not seen, although he seemed to anticipate them with great agility.

Suddenly, she felt electricity surge through her. She knew that familiar pain from her days in training. She had been stunned with a stun gun. With all her might, she fought the immediate sensation, but was unable to fight the second zap as the woman let her have it again.

Romia dropped to the floor.

Chapter 26

"Damn, Keliegh, what ran over you?" Lawrence asked, seeing that Keliegh was truly awake, up, and ready to leave. From what he'd been told, he expected Keliegh to be two sheets to the wind on pain meds, or all strapped up in traction. Keliegh was badly bruised and his head had a large bandage above his brow. His face looked as if he'd lost a few rounds to a heavyweight boxer.

Keliegh shook his head. There was no way he wanted to talk about the encounter with the Shadow. There was no way he wanted to even think about the implications he had posed. Romia never would have been behind something so sinister. She never would have backed such activities. What connection did she have with someone like that?

"And to threaten me," Keliegh said under his breath.

"What?" Lawrence said, gathering Keliegh's paperwork from the duty nurse. There was no way he could drive.

Keliegh looked at his uncle. "Nothing," he lied.

"Now, you said something. Who threatened you?" Lawrence asked, moving them from earshot of the nurse.

"Some punk-ass ninja in black tights, that's who."

"Punk-ass ninja? Well, I see he beat you to a pulp. Backed that threat smmooove up didn't he, haha."

"No . . . now there you're wrong. Well, I mean, you're right, but you're wrong. I was trying to have a civil conversation with him about Romia Smith and he just . . ." Keliegh began, attempting to flail his arms around, but the badly sprained one didn't move.

"He could have killed you. Easily, from what the doctor said. Now, tell me from the start, who did this?"

"He wasn't trying to kill me. He was trying to scare me. Told me to . . ." Keliegh looked at his cell phone noticing two missed calls from Tommy. He called her number. "Back off finding Romia," he said, finishing his conversation.

"Hello." It was Kiki Turner, Tommy's half sister. He knew her voice. She had answered Tommy's cell phone.

"Hey, where is Tommy?"

"She's in the hospital. She was attacked by Romia."

"What?" Keliegh gasped.

"She said she was attacked by Romia. That she went to Romia's place to meet up with this Maxwell Huntington. It was a trap and Romia was waiting and tried to kill her. Just beat the devil out of her, too. She's in the hospital. She's got a broken ankle, a concussion. I'm about to get some charges pressed. Why hasn't anyone issued any warrants against this Romia person? You've got a swoon out there and—"

"Swerve," Keliegh corrected.

"What the hell ever! You've got this cop out there killing people and running amuck with no explanation and—"

"I have an explanation."

"Well, tell me!"

"What room is Tommy in?"

"I'll come to you," Kiki blurted.

"No, I'm in the hospital too. I'll come to Tommy's room." Keliegh said, realizing his pain meds were wearing thin. He flinched at the pain in his ribs.

Chapter 27

Maybe Jim just had a way with people, but it just always seemed easy for him to get information that others seemed to find impossible to access. After a morning of seeing their hard work wasted, Jim wasn't about to just let it go without more information. He didn't understand how Lawrence could. Nothing was fitting. And now Keliegh had been put in the hospital and Tommy too. It was a bit too coincidental that they had been put out of commission like that. Lawrence had called him right after finding out about Keliegh. Jim ran on a hunch and tried to contact Tommy, and that's how he found out she was out of the way as well. He beat it to the hospital and had a few words with her before her sister came in and busted up the party.

She hadn't said much, but it was enough to make Jim wonder about this case a little harder. "Who are they gonna go after next? Me? Lawrence? I wish someone would just try it," he growled under his breath. He was frustrated. He hated when things didn't add up. "Why do we always get the weird cases?" he asked himself.

It always seemed that way for him and his partner. Dangerous liaisons with gay serial killers, mad scientists trying to steal body organs, people who were supposed to be dead and yet managing to commit murders. "What next?" he asked rhetorically, not really wanting to know the answer. "Aliens?"

Hairy Mary grinned at him broadly, flirtatiously, before leaving him alone with the micro-files he'd requested. He wanted to see those that aged back to around the time Romia was born. He was going to figure out who this woman, Romia, was first before making a decision on whether she was guilty of mass murder with her bare hands.

That small piece of fabric found on the scene intrigued him. It was out of place. It was obvious by the way Keliegh's expression changed that he'd seen it before. "Had to belong to Romia," Jim deduced, speaking in an undertone. "And it has to mean something or why would a woman like her, in the position she was in, have it on her?"

Jim scoured the files, looking for any cases where there was an image of a phoenix or anything phoenix related. Ten years ago, twenty years ago, twenty-five and beyond, he looked, until, finally, he found it in a micro-file that was around thirty years ago.

"Geez," he sighed while reading the file, running his fingers through his scruffy hair. He looked around, hoping no one was watching him. What he was reading had to have been top-secret information at one time. Scrolling the window back to the introduction page of the electronic file, he saw it was titled, "The Phoenix Team." The next page was a scanned-in document that had a red stamp that read "Confidential: CIA."

Holding the photo he'd taken of the tapestry piece, he scrolled through the pages of the file. He was looking for any lead, or something within one of the photos that came close to matching the fabric. There had to be a reason Romia Smith treasured it beyond the obvious.

The Phoenix team did special work for the US government. They were selected for their highly sensitive abilities. "Amazing," Jim mumbled, reading what each member could do. "Holy moly, all we need now are a few circus midgets and we'd have a full-blown act," he huffed, reading on. "So why kill them off? They seem pretty helpful . . . ooh," he said, noticing

the big read letters that read, "Terrorist?" His eyes widened
with the discovery. "That word wasn't even a buzzword back
then," he mumbled. "I didn't even realize they were using it
back then."

Clearly, as he read on, he discovered that the US wasn't
the only government eventually to put them to use. The members eventually became assassins for hire. Soon they were shut
down by the very government that created them.

The leader, the Phoenix, was dead. They'd raided his lair
and killed all there. Apparently, there were members of this
elite group of spies who were still at large. Each member of the
team had a bio, well, the dead ones anyway. "Who's looking
for them? Anybody looking for them?" Jim asked in an undertone, looking through the rest of the information quickly. It
was common for him to talk to himself when sorting thoughts
in his head. Looking around nervously, he was starting to feel
antsy, as if he might be learning too much. "All members of
the group are presumed dead . . . right, I really believe that,
and I'm sure so do those who are after them now." He read
on about how proud the government was to "close this case."
"Closed case only means one thing: they are not all dead and
this case is far from closed. It means to me that those living
are the mercy of bounty hunters and mercenaries. Wow." He
read on. "And I can't imagine them just taking this kinda
thing lying down."

Just then, he saw the photos of the dead. All were slain
execution style, violent and with a bit of overkill. Finally, coming upon one of a dark-haired woman, he could see that she'd
been shot multiple times, and photographed sprawled face
up, in a pool of blood on the floor of a sparsely furnished
apartment. "Massacre, my God." Jim sighed. "That's one way
to keep a government secret. Kill everyone they think might
know it."

With a closer look at the photo, something caught his eye.

It was on the wall of the apartment, hanging in a frame. Two clicks of the mouse bought the picture clearer into view.

"Bingo!" Jim exploded.

Just then, he was interrupted.

"Excuse me, but who are you and who gave you authorization to view these files?" a suit asked. Jim quickly closed the file and shoved the photo in his jacket pocket.

He stood.

"I asked you a question, Detective Beem."

"You know me?"

"We know everyone who comes in here. Believe that," the suit sneered, pushing him out of the way and taking over the computer, hoping to retrieve what Jim was just viewing. "That picture?" he asked, requesting Jim hand it over. Jim obeyed. The suit looked at it and smirked.

"Everybody seems interested in this case lately."

"I'm not the only one wanting information?"

"Nope, but you won't find anything either. This case"—the young man twisted his face smugly—"nothing more than an embarrassing witch hunt," he assured.

Jim chuckled with a sarcastic air chasing his laughter. "Well, yeah, had to be, because if they were witches, you'd have never caught 'em. By the looks of those bloody scenes, you caught 'em and killed them."

"Exactly, we got 'em," he said, pointing at the computer. "They're gone. This case is closed."

"Really?"

"Yeah. Just a group of would-be terrorists. Government shut 'em down years ago. Don't know what's got them in the news again, but oh well. You're chasing shadows."

"Funny you should call them that." Jim snickered, thinking about what Tommy had called her attacker.

"Yeah, well, that's the deal," the suit said, as if ending their conversation.

The suit fanned his hand toward the door, as if offering Jim a way out. Jim looked at the door and then back at the well-groomed young man. "Okay, but before I go, let me ask you this: who's Maxwell Huntington?"

"Okay, I'll play. Who *was* Maxell Huntington?"

"Was?"

Chapter 28

Romia felt stiff and exhausted. The fight was nearly gone but not quite. They must have known she wasn't completely spent, and that was probably why now she was tied up. She watched silently as the small group of foreigners spoke their indistinguishable language while packing up their apparent hideout under the church.

Why here? Romia pondered, remembering her childhood and the days this church was visited by her at her mother's side. She would play in the pews while her mother confessed. Never once did she even imagine her mother to be capable of sin. Never could she fathom her mother being capable of anything that would have warranted murder.

"You're all liars," Romia mumbled just as the youngest of the group—the bushy-headed one who had appeared to her as a shadow in the night, sparring, fighting, besting her, for now—walked past. He glanced at her. He'd been packing with intent, not engaging in much small talk. They had computers and files, more than she first realized. They had a full-blown office here in the basement of this church. It was apparently headquarters for their little organization.

"I never lie," he said in English, yet with a strong accent. "I have no reason to," he added, continuing to pack the boxes.

"Then tell me why I'm here. Why you've toyed with me, kidnapped me. Set me up as a murderer, ruined my life. Why did you send people to kill me?" Romia begged for those answers now.

"Now, there you're wrong. Those men came on their own and you decided on your own to kill them," the Shadow explained. "Which was a mistake, by the way," he added, all but rolling his eyes. "All you did was draw attention to yourself, and us," he spat angrily as if he'd had a bad day.

"They were going to kill me!" Romia explained.

"Perhaps! But your timing couldn't have been worse."

"Royale!" Maxwell snapped. "You can talk on the plane. We don't have much time."

Romia jerked at the restraints. "Plane? I'm not getting on a plane."

"Shut up, you little whiner," the woman snapped at her in the foreign accent.

Romia hissed at her, surprising herself with the response. These people were bringing out a side of her she didn't realize was there.

The woman laughed.

"Yes, you are getting on a plane. We're taking you home," Maxwell explained, coming between the two of them. "I know this all seems insane to you right now, but by morning you'll know the truth and, if you are loyal, you will join us."

"And if I'm not?" Romia growled.

"Then you will die at my hands," Maxwell said without flinching. His words caught the attention of the others in the room. It was clear his words were true, and powerful. Romia stared into his eyes, and in her belly she felt it. She felt truth. What he said he truly planned to carry out. He was a leader and an influential one.

Chapter 29

Kiki wasn't about to let Keliegh or Lawrence get near Tommy. "She's sedated and you're not gonna get anything outta her right now. I'm her attorney and it ain't happ'nin', boys. Not until I talk to her first."

"Fine!" Keliegh blurted in frustration. "Look, Kiki, we don't have all night!"

Lawrence stood between them. "Ms. Porter, you'll have to excuse my nephew. He needs sedation. Let's go," Lawrence said in Keliegh's direction. Keliegh stormed out of the room in a huff.

Leaving the hospital, Lawrence called Jim.

"What's our next move?" Keliegh asked.

"Well, as much as I don't want to do this, Jim thinks we need to pay Ms. Romia's apartment a visit."

"Why?"

"He said we'd talk there. He's being all super-spy and secretive."

When Keliegh and Lawrence reached Romia's apartment, they found the door ajar. They didn't have time to wait for asearch warrant. *What were they looking for anyway?* Keliegh didn't know.

"Now, don't get crazy," Lawrence began, "but Jim got in to see Tommy before her watchdog showed up. He said Tommy said whoever worked her over was waiting."

"Well, yeah, I got back to my place and homeboy was on my sofa. So there are two of them and I have a feeling both were planted."

"Planted? And who would want you two out of the game like that? Who would risk assault charges to do this?" Lawrence asked.

"Maxwell Huntington, and trust me, that guy couldn't care less about an assault charge."

Lawrence gawked at Keliegh. "Maxwell Hunt . . . the IA guy?"

"He's not IA," Jim chimed in. "Unless he's the walking dead. Maxwell Huntington died over twenty years ago, and he was white."

Lawrence now gawked at his partner. "Wait! When did you find out?"

"Today. So I was doing some checking around on this case. I mean, truthfully, did you think it was kosher the way Cap'n just took us off that case and gave it to the feds?"

"The feds got the case?" Keliegh asked.

"No. I called a personal friend there and she didn't have a clue what I was talking about," Jim continued. "Red flag number two."

"Well, feds lie," Lawrence said with a smirk.

"Not my pet fed, she wouldn't lie to me," Jim said, smiling slyly. "They don't have it."

"Anyway," Lawrence said, rolling his eyes. "So what we got?"

"Nothing here," Keliegh said before noticing the front door. He was closely examining the doorjamb. It was obvious the lock had been jimmied. "Well, maybe nothing. I didn't notice this the first time."

"What first time?"

"I came here once already, but I had a key so it was legit. The place was trashed. Like it is now, but the lock was not jimmied." He tried his key. It no longer fit. "Why would she spring her own lock?"

"Good question." Jim took a closer look at the lock. Just then, Lawrence pulled everyone's attention to the box of pictures he found overturned.

"Who is this?" Lawrence asked, holding up a picture of Romia and a man.

Keliegh looked closer. His heart began to pound. "Damn! It's the dude from The Spot. Shit," he sighed, running his fingers through his thick hair. It was in need of a cut but he hoped nobody noticed. Besides, at a moment like this when he realized the woman he loved—and, yes, he loved Romia— could be possibly lying to him about knowing the man she had shot, she was taking precedence in his thoughts.

The man in the picture with her was in uniform, smiling, with his arm around Romia's waist. There was no mistaking this picture. This was a happiness/togetherness pose. There was no mistaking the dude, either; it was the guy from the tavern. Keliegh had gotten a good view of him when he bumped Romia.

"Who is it? Old boyfriend?" Jim asked, sounding casual, looking over Lawrence's shoulder at the photo.

"No, it's the man she shot." Keliegh sighed. "She doesn't know this guy. I know she doesn't know this guy," he went on.

"You apparently don't know anything," Lawrence said. Both Jim and Lawrence reared back dramatically, as if in a conjoined ah-ha moment. "We got ourselves a swerve, boys," Lawrence then announced.

"What do we do now?" Keliegh answered, sounding beaten.

"We find Romia," Jim answered. "Lawrence is right, Keliegh, Romia has swerved, but not the way you think." He pointed at Lawrence. "But, still, we need to find her and find her fast."

"Dammit!" Keliegh exclaimed, grabbing his sore arm as if suddenly remembering the pain in it, or transferring the pain from his heart to it.

Chapter 30

Romia sat quietly on the plane. She'd never flown before. There were many things she had not done outside of being a cop and fighting in the ring. She was nearly thirty, and she'd not been to Disneyland, she'd not eaten cotton candy, she'd never had sex, nor had she ever been on a flight, and this one was to be over eighteen hours.

Always do it big when you do it, she reasoned.

She was on her way to the Europe. She fought emotion and confusion and all sorts of other feelings. Her head was full of new information and her loyalties were in question.

No one had stopped them, or questioned them at the airport. Apparently, there was no APB in effect yet, or not one that was being paid attention to. *It wasn't as if she'd made national news. She'd killed someone who wasn't even dead. How serious of a crime could that be?*

"You have a mission, and it's not to waste your life being a cop," Maxwell had said to her in the car on the way to the airport. She glanced over at him. He seemed more relaxed that they were on their way to the plane.

It was a private charter and very comfortable and expensive looking. She'd seen this type of plane in movies, but never dreamed she'd be on one. The young man, Royale, had wandered back, from who knows where, to his seat. He had a bottle of water in his hand and some kind of sandwich. She watched him. He moved like a dancer. Smooth and charming, his lips turned into a clearly unconscious smile. His eyes danced with devilment and mystery, and maybe a little bit of danger, too. He was distracting to her. It wasn't that she found him attractive, with his sandy blond locks and green eyes. No, she didn't see anything attractive about him, not really. He was just disturbing.

Who was she trying to fool? Hell, he was beautiful, and she couldn't keep her eyes off him.

Chapter 31

The Phoenix: Ten years ago

"Someone is apparently trying to kill me," the Phoenix said with a wicked smile curving his full lips. His steel-like blue eyes were not moving, not flinching in the least.

It was a longtime put-off meeting between the two of them, taking place off the coast of France.

He had avoided speaking with the Phoenix for years, as he knew it would mean continued affiliation with him, and he was tired of it. He wanted to be free of it.

He was dead now, and so how much freer could he be?

Looking now at the Phoenix's tired face, however, he regretted his thoughts. There would be no freedom from this man, not as long as they shared blood.

"Why would someone want you dead?" was all he could ask.

"I've lived a very long life, and what a full life it's been, too. I'm thinking that along the line I've apparently pissed some people off. Finding out whom specifically has become a real challenge, however." The Phoenix chuckled slightly, snapping his fingers for the waiter to bring him another lemon for his Perrier. "I have my thoughts on the matter. I will never understand a person who uses his mind and its potential for such a wasted effort as revenge. It's such a useless endeavor."

He looked around cautiously and then back, only to meet the Phoenix's unworried face. "You don't need to worry here, we're quite safe. Haven't I always kept you safe?"

"No," he answered bluntly, thinking of *Capri*, but before he could say the name . . . "Speaking of safe, how are the wife and the children?" the Phoenix asked.

It had taken a long time for the Phoenix to accept that he had gone against his orders and married a civilian and had children with her.

Civilian. Always at war, he thought, noticing the tension in the tone of the Phoenix's inquiry. He just smiled, knowing the question was a hard one for the Phoenix to ask.

"The wife is well and so are the children," he answered. "Safe," he added confidently and with a little dig in it.

"So your life with her has been better than your life with me?" the Phoenix asked.

He looked off; he couldn't believe where this conversation was going. "I don't understand why you asked me that." he said. "You have always been in everything I do. You act like I've ever been Phoenix free. You act as though my marriage now has been Phoenix free," he growled. "I wouldn't be here if you weren't in my life. You are in all of our lives. Why are you even talking about my wife? I don't want to talk about my wife," he said, abruptly shutting down the conversation.

The Phoenix sipped his water before tipping the waiter and sending him on his way. "Let's get back to the issue at hand then: my life. As you of all people should know, betrayal runs deep among us. I believe my coordinates have been compromised."

"And you think I—"

"No. Of course not. I think another traitor is in our midst."

"Another one," he repeated.

The Phoenix laughed sarcastically. "You are far too sensitive, my son," the Phoenix said.

It caused a chill to carry up his spine. It was rare that the Phoenix addressed him as his son. It was true, but often not mentioned and, now, far from noteworthy. There had been too many years, too much water under the bridge for him to care about his legacy with this man.

The Phoenix sipped his water again after squeezing in the juice of the lemon wedge and dropping the rind in. "By the way, when will I ever get to see my grandchildren? You don't think I'm worthy of seeing them?"

"No! I don't want you near my children. They are normal and happy children. They have no idea of the blood that flows in their veins and I'll be damned if I'll ever tell them!" He spoke in Arabic now.

"Oh, they'll find out. I promise you that."

Chapter 32

The plane was flying smoothly, much like an expensive car. Romia still found it impossible to sleep.

"Are you going to try to sleep?" Maxwell asked.

"No," she answered. The tension in her voice was obvious.

He smiled. "You should."

"I'll never sleep again," she said, sounding almost dramatic. Still, she watched Royale out of one eye. He was now settling in to a catnap.

"You and Royale are finished fighting for one day, I'm sure," Maxwell said, obviously noting her eyes.

"I don't like him."

"One day you'll change your mind," Maxwell assured.

"I never will."

"You're very stubborn."

Finally, she rolled her eyes in his direction and sighed copiously. "Tell me what's going on. You've explained very little to me. Okay, so I get that you're the good guys, or so you say, but I—"

Maxwell held up his finger to silence her. "I'll talk. You listen."

Upon those words, Romia noticed even Royale's eyes crack open slightly. He too had questions about their mission. Romia could tell.

Chapter 33

The Phoenix

The Phoenix appeared by all rights to be a myth. Yet, top secret and reluctantly discussed, he was real. Although he was a certifiable genius, to some he was a certifiably madman, overlooking authority, finding his way of thinking to be superior to the US government.

Forming a small team of those much like him, he and his group often came in uninvited, did what was usually unasked, and left taking more gifts than were offered. Young, strong, trained in martial warfare and destruction, this group of loyal followers made it their goal to right all wrongs and wrong some rights at the discretion of their leader, the Phoenix. Making leadership decisions based on his moral and self-developed loyalties, he began using this team in ways the government did not intend to use them.

Viewed by many as thieves, assassins, and vigilantes, their purpose for involvement in certain situations seemed driven only by the self-need, and greed, of their leader.

Those who followed him never questioned his word, as they were birds of a feather.

Not only did he have a high IQ, but it was rumored that the Phoenix, which was the only name he answered to, also had physical peculiarities unusual to most people. The Phoenix was indeed a hybrid. He sought out young children who were much like him in many ways—gifted. He raised them as foster children for the most part, teaching them to hone their extraordinary abilities until finally they, too, had mastery over their intellectual and kinetic abilities. It was believed that he trained them through the use of much mind control, as they looked to him as more than a father. They, for the most part, worshipped him.

His brand of leadership eventually led to internal conflicts and strife as well, and soon they were a household divided. Those who bucked his leadership took on their own missions. They were based more in immediate and material gratification than those of increased power and stroking of the Phoenix's ego. Those who transgressed the Phoenix crossed lines they should not have, and made dangerous alliances. It was these crossed allegiances and disloyalties that made him and his group a liability.

Once the breaches were identified, behind closed doors governments met jointly to use those breaches against them to seek and destroy them. Unable to pin down the government to which he was truly affiliated, all sovereignties seemed to want this Phoenix and all those associated with him gone. The Phoenix, as if sensing his demise, dispersed the group.

The chase to find them all and destroy them was daunting, with them being always one step ahead of their would-be captures. Many escaped capture, some did not. Some of those who did not get captured became traitors in order to save their own lives.

Even after all these years, there remained those who would hunt the survivors for a hefty bounty. The biggest prize, of course, would be in finding the Phoenix himself.

Chapter 34

Jim, after dropping off Keliegh and Lawrence, went out to the hospital to see Tommy. It was easy to get in. The badge came in handy when he wanted it to. She'd had surgery on her ankle and was resting "Hey," he said to her, noticing that the curtain around her was open. She was watching TV.

Quickly, she pointed the remote and clicked it off. "Hey," she said, looking a little embarrassed. Her hair was messy and she looked a little pasty in color, no doubt leftover drug effects from her surgical procedure.

"Got some information on our friend Romia."

"Like what?"

"Well . . ." Jim hesitated. "Okay, I'll try it on you before I try it out on Lawrence and Keliegh. It's some wild shit and, well, they won't believe it, but you might."

"Why? Because I'm female," she answered, frowning just a little bit."

Jim smiled. "Yeah, you're female. I had noticed that a while back and was thinking, okay, so if there's anything I want to try on a female—she's the one," he said, trying to keep the flirt from his voice.

It didn't work, as Tommy quickly ran her fingers through her messy hair and cleared her throat. "Okay, try me."

"Would love to," he said, again not meaning to come on strong, but failing. "Ahem . . . sorry," he added. "What do I got . . . um, okay. Let me start at the beginning. You know anything about like . . . heightened sensory perceptions or like . . ."

"Like ESP?"

"Well, more than that. I mean, like David Copperfield or Houdini, shit like that."

"Well, no. I mean, they do magic tricks."

"But not everybody can do that shit. I mean, I know a few card tricks, but what they do is amazing. I saw Copperfield live one time in Vegas and he was amazing."

"Okay, go on."

"Well, what if you had, like, dozens of Copperfields or Houdinis working for you—spying for you?"

"Shit, I'd be unstoppable. Well, unless one of them shot me, then I'd have to call on my *Matrix* skills. But you didn't say I had those skills," she added. She was playing along well and catching on quick to the gist of the conversation and where he was taking it. She was quick. He liked that.

"Exactly. But other than getting shot or stabbed or . . . "

"Or leap a building in a single bound."

"Yeah, shit like that, you could basically get in, get out, and do whatever you wanted to a government file or even take out somebody who wasn't expecting you to show up in the middle of the night, like a ninja, without the average person being able to stop you."

"So you're saying we're dealing with a buncha Houdini assassins."

"We were. Most of them are dead."

"Romia?"

"Her mother."

"Her mother was Houdini?"

"I think so. I think she was part of a team of Houdini ninja people who had these"—Jim ran his hands over his body as if to represent something going on inside him, uncontrollably moving around inside him like ants—"these abilities. They were like like hybrids."

"Wow! Unbelievable."

He turned away. "I told you."

"No, no, I believe you. I'm just saying wow. I mean, that woman who kicked my ass, she got on the phone, and a second after she'd pretended to be Romia, she was me."

"You?"

"Yeah, she had my voice and everything. I mean, I was out, but I wasn't, like, *out* out. I could hear her. She had my voice."

"Well, then, she's definitely one of them. I haven't quite figured out what they want, but they are definitely putting their little cult together and they need Romia." Jim looked around for a chair and slid it close to the bed and sat down. "I think the government thinks they cleaned up a mess it made, but, as always, they didn't do a good job of it and now it's back to haunt them."

"'Kay, and Romia?"

"She's a pawn. I think she's a part of it but doesn't know it—well, she may know now, but even then I can't believe she's being told the truth. If she's as good a cop as I've always heard, she can't be going along willingly."

"You think they're blackmailing her. I mean, they did set her up pretty good with that murder frame. I'm sure it was a setup now."

"Well, it appears so. But what I'm thinking is that her mother was in it deep, and for some reason they think Romia is like a chip off the off black magic box." Jim pulled out the picture of the phoenix tapestry. "This symbol is a key."

"Romia wore that on her jacket like a crest."

"And in a way it was. I'm sure it was for her mother, anyway. But in Romia's case, it was a target. She was a walking bull's-eye for these guys. I mean, they aren't stupid, they probably knew she existed all along, but . . ." Jim shook his head. "But she didn't help the situation by drawing their attention to herself. They probably assumed she knew what the bird symbolized, or that she was telling them, 'Yeah, I gots abilities.'"

"Tell me more about these abilities, because Romia creeps me out sometimes. You telling me she inherited them?"

"I think so. From what I read from her mother's bio and the others, their abilities are like what anyone could have but focused on, or built on, they can cause a bend in the norm."

"Like, speed or like . . ."

"Yeah, like one dude's bio said he was a pyro . . . pryo . . . he could start fires with his brain. You ever hear of such a thing?"

"Yeah, pyrokinetics, they set fires. Spontaneous combustion has been the source of many scientific studies . . . not proven, of course. Usually it's a trick, like rain dancing, but still, you gotta be damn good at it so as not to kill yourself."

"Okay, well, then, you won't think this is crazy. Romia's mom was a sharpshooter and trained in martial arts and all the regular stuff, but supposedly she also had telekinetic abilities. Like she could read minds and like . . . like scramble somebody's brain . . . like . . . hypnotize. Yeah, she supposedly was mentally bent that way."

"Wow, so you think Romia inherited that?"

"I think Romia's mother set her up to fall right into that bend. She didn't die when Romia was six years old. She died a few years ago—gunned down."

"Damn." Tommy gulped in surprise. "Are you sure?"

"That's what it showed in the report. The government went after everyone on the Phoenix Team and killed them. You know how it is when you're different. These people knew too much. They were a threat to national security."

"Damn. But if you're saying Romia's mother set Romia up to have the same 'abilities' that got her killed, she was setting Romia up for the same people to come after her. How could she set Romia up for a life like that?"

"I'm not sure it went that way. Whoever raised Romia, maybe they knew her mother, maybe they didn't."

"If they did, they had to know that Romia could possibly have the same mental predisposition and sensitivities. Something musta given it away."

"Maybe it was Romia kicking ass on the playground at six years old or walking through walls and shit!"

Tommy laughed, but then again gathered the seriousness of the potential situation. "So whoever it was has probably been watching Romia a long-ass time, just waiting for the right moment. But still, who? If all these people are dead—"

"Tommy, I'm not sure any of these people are really dead. I'm not even sure Romia's mother is dead. The guy called it a witch hunt and . . ."

"And if they are what they think they are . . ."

"Exactly, they wouldna been able to stop 'em—not all of 'em."

"So what do you think they're up to? Those who didn't get caught?"

"I think they want freedom, peace, to be left alone . . . or, who knows, maybe they want to take over the world. I think they want a lot of things. But I also think there could be some of them who just want straight-up revenge, a payback for the 'thank you for your service, here's a bullet in your head' the government gave them."

"But how does this really connect Romia?"

"Romia isn't just one of them, that I know—"

"How?"

"I got a hunch and my hunches are never wrong."

"So, who is Romia?"

"I have a sneaking suspicion she's real close to the Phoenix himself. I just got a gut feeling from a couple of things I read in the report. Also, think about it, why would they come after her if she wasn't?"

"Wish she hadn't killed those guys from outta town. They coulda at least told us why they were after her. Who were they anyway?"

"Don't know, but I want to put my money on mercenaries."

"Hmmm. And Maxwell Huntington?"

Jim nodded. "Not sure about his side of the fence, either. But I do know he's using Romia to help his cause and I'm pretty sure it's a cause that isn't coming from a patriotic duty."

"So you believe she's innocent, huh?"

Jim smiled. "Yeah. I do."

"Me too. Especially now," Tommy said, pointing to her cast leg up in the sling.

"So, what do you think's gonna happen next?" she asked after a moment of silence between them.

"I think it's a repeat of history, only this time the good guys aren't gonna be in charge."

"As if they ever were."

"Exactly."

Chapter 35

Maxwell continued to tell her more, much more. He told her what was not found in the files. "So now you know."

"So you're telling me that my mother was a spy. That she was some kind of international assassin?" Romia said, almost laughing out loud.

Maxwell nodded. "And so much more."

"What more? Are you saying she was traitor to this Phoenix person or are you saying she was a traitor to the government?" Romia now gave in to the laughter. "You're crazy. What kind of madness is this?" she went on. "What kind of fool are you? This story is madness," she said, feeling hysteria growing. "And has nothing to do with me."

"Romia, listen to me." Maxwell retrieved the brief case he carried and again pulled out the manila folder that contained the photos. He pulled out the one of the woman. "This is your mother. She was murdered for being a member of the Phoenix family. You have to believe me. She was a cold-blooded killer hired by the government to resolve matters of national security before she became a loose cannon—a swerve, as you cops call it."

Romia stared at the photo before ripping it from his hands for a closer look. "This can't be my mother. This woman is too old to be my mother. My mother died over twenty years ago. She was a young woman, a girl, when she died. She was hit by a car. We were together and she was hit by a car! This woman is clearly in her forties."

Romia's eyes burned as if onions had been rubbed into them. Again, she studied the picture. The facial features looked similar, but there was no way this woman was her mother. She had watched her mother go over the hood of that car. She saw her die. "She was blond, for crying out loud."

Quickly biting her knuckles to keep from crying out, Romia threw the picture and turned toward the window. "That's not my mother," she blurted. "She would have contacted me. She would have wanted to make me know she was alive. No matter her position with the government, she would not have abandoned me."

At that, Maxwell shook the picture toward her. "Yes, she may have tried to warn you about what was to come of you just for being her daughter."

"My being her daughter means what exactly?"

"There are many out there waiting for just the moment that you would come of age, and realized of who you are, so as to kill you."

Romia, now with eyes blazing, turned to him. She fought the question that burned in her mind. If she were to believe this story, if she were to give in for just one more moment, she knew she must now ask the obvious. Her eyes fought with her brain to look at the picture of her mother again. Her eyes won out. After staring at the photo for a minute or two, she quickly turned away. "Who am I?"

"You are a threat."

Romia's head spun back to him. "A threat to who? The government? Hardly."

"You are a threat to those who wish to rebuild the Phoenix legacy."

"Why?"

"Because the Phoenix is your father, and right now, you're on the opposite side of the fence. Which is where you want to be, however, your being there is a threat to those who want to keep that legacy alive, and you are a target to those who seek to destroy it."

"You're crazy. First you tell me my mother was a spy and then you tell me that my father is the leader of some international cult spy gang? You're insane."

"Haven't you ever wondered who your father is?"

"No," Romia lied. Her eyes then caught Royale's in a gaze that was nothing less than hynoptic. It was as if he, too, had wondered similar things about his own life.

"Fine. Listen. I've been at this a long time. We have to stop these people. We have to find the remainders of the team and bring them to justice. The leader is your father. You have to help me find him. You have to gain his trust and then lead him to me. You have to trust me," Maxwell said, shoving the pictures roughly back into the folder that was nestled in the soft leather briefcase.

"Oh my God, that's a laugh. First you have golden boy here kick my ass, then you frame me for murder, then you beat the snot outta my . . ." She stammered, "my friends. and you want me to trust you? You haven't given me any information. All you've given me is a fairy tale, which, by the way, I don't believe."

"Haven't you ever wondered about the things you can do? Your abilities? Oh, yes." He nodded excitedly. "I've watched you for years. I've followed you. As soon as I realized who you were, I followed you. You're just like her in so many ways."

"Like who? My mother? What abilities?"

"Romia. You are the only one who can help him."

"Him?"

Maxwell nodded. "You need to convince him to turn himself in. He'll trust you."

Romia looked at Royale and at the man and woman who had now come into the cabin where they had been listening to Maxwell explaining their assignment. She sighed heavily, showing her confusion. "Turn himself in? Help him?"

"They are going to kill you otherwise. Those men who came after you, he sent them. Right now, not knowing where your loyalties are, you're a threat to him and he's a threat to national security."

"You're bounty hunters. You're after." The light suddenly came on. "You're after my father. You're saying my father is the Phoenix. That has to be what you're saying to me. That has to be why those men called me that." She chuckled out loud, repeating what she'd heard, only in her own words now, assimilated through her own thoughts. "You're saying my mother was a part of this team and she was murdered because of it. You're saying that they are some . . . some weirdos with some 'talents' that are, like, unusual, and that makes them extra dangerous or useful to the government who hired them. Like a missile that they were sorry they built, and now they want to dismantle, so they hired you to kill them all. Ooh, but they are fighting back and you can't stop 'em."

"Romia. Listen to me. Your father and those he's brought into his fold are powerful, more powerful than you can imagine. I'm not trying to hurt him. I'm trying to stop him before they go too far. The government is trying to stop them. They are haywire."

"Swerves," she said, with a sneer coming to her words. He nooded. "No . . ." She balked, growing uncomfortable in her seat. "You find him yourself."

"No. You're going to help me. Now, we're the good guys and—"

"You're not. You want to kill my father, and you probably killed my mother and . . ." Romia stood. "You want me to betray my father so that you can kill him just like you killed my mother. I can't help you."

"Romia you're wrong," Maxwell said looking up at her.

She glanced over at Royale in search of confirmation of Maxwell's story. She couldn't find it. She only saw confusion in his eyes. He was just like her. For whatever reason, he too had been brought into Maxwell's trust as an unwitting participant in his hunt for the Phoenix—her father. *What is Royale's connection to all of this?* she wondered. She fell upon her wits now, for they were all she had. "Does it matter if I believe you?"

"What are your options?" Maxwell asked.

Suddenly, Romia felt a cold chill run through her. "I can go back and tell the truth."

Maxwell grinned wickedly. "Romia, you can never go back. As we speak they are forming a posse to find you and to take you in. They are planning to prosecute you for first-degree murder and assault on two fellow officers. You are a lethal weapon. You're armed and dangerous just by existing. They won't hesitate to kill you on sight. If you think you had hard time believing this story, you just try to run it by a judge who was paid to put that confidential file out of his mind and out of existence."

"Keliegh would never believe that I'm a killer. He—" she began.

"He what? He loves you? Not anymore." The woman chuckled in a nasty fashion before leaving the cabin for the front of the plane where she had been previously. She appeared bored with the whole situation. This was just a job to her, that Romia could tell. Who knew how many other of her "family" this woman had been a part of tricking into Maxwell's snare, only to be betrayed and possibly murdered without a trial for their crimes against the system—or worse—for their crimes of being "different."

"What did you do?" Romia asked the woman.

"I did magic," she said in broken English.

Romia stepped up to her. "Did you kill him?"

"Does it matter? You'll be just as dead soon."

Chapter 36

Two weeks passed quickly for those left to wonder about Romia Smith. There hadn't been a sight or sound out of her. Even Keliegh had to confess that he was disappointed by her silence.

The story of the Phoenix and his team wasn't just strange trivia to Tommy. All she could think was that if it had been that easy for Jim to gather the information, how much easier would it befor someone with murder on his mind? How could anyone with that intent not see the connection between this group and Romia Smith? A simple cross-reference of Romia, her date of birth, and a few preserved documents would bring that all together. "Killed by a bounty hunter? So it was murder," Tommy mumbled under her breath, thinking aloud about Romia's mother. She had taken all that Jim had told her he'd found, and now was putting it in her own mind the way she understood it.

Maybe Romia is out for revenge. Maybe she found out who killed her mother and all this is about revenge. Does that make sense, Tommy? This woman was a good cop. She was unconcerned about the life she knew nothing about, right?

Knocking hard on the door, Tommy waited for an answer. There was none, just the muffled sound of distant conversation. She listened hard at the door. She could hear the voice of a woman speaking. She knocked again. Slowly, it opened. The older woman looked shy and reserved.

"Hello, I'd like to speak with you for a moment." She

flashed her badge quickly, as was her common way. No one needed to know her name, and she rarely exposed her badge long enough for anyone to find it out.

The woman stared hard at her. "About what? I've not broken the law."

"No, you haven't, but I have to ask you some questions."

"About what? I've not witnessed any crimes, either."

"Oh, I think you did. It was just a little over twenty years ago. The woman's name was Capri."

The woman's eyes grew wide but she didn't slam the door as Tommy expected she would. She was older, and probably contemplated an escape should she need to do such a thing. There would be no getting away for her. Tommy wasn't aware that the woman's eyes were as bad as they were, but soon she came to realize that she couldn't escape if she wanted to.

"I'm not Capri," the woman admitted. Looking up and down the hallway, she looked Tommy up and down. "I knew her. I told her one day this plan would fall short, but she wanted to do it. Did you know her? My God." The woman gasped. "Of course you do. You're Romia."

Tommy contemplated the lie. "Yes."

"Well, of course you would be. She told me one day you'd come looking for me." The woman stood back from the door to allow Tommy entrance.

Tommy entered the apartment.

"She did?"

"She said that one day you'd need to see me. She said you'd want answers."

"Yes," Tommy played along. She'd hit pay dirt and wasn't about to let the woman know she wasn't Romia. "Have you watched the news?"

"No. I'm legally blind so I can't read or watch television. But I listen. I've heard on the news they're looking for you."

"Yes, they are."

"And they won't stop until they find you. They didn't stop until they found Capri, bless her heart. She used to tell me all the time they were looking for her. I thought she was a little . . ."—the woman swirled her fingers around her ears—"that is, until they killed her."

"When is the last time you saw Ca . . ." Tommy hesitated. "My mother?"

"Child, she's been dead for years. You were there."

"Well, I have my suspicions about everything now. I don't believe anything about my life. The report I read said you were my mother so . . ."

The woman cackled. "I was too old then to be your mother and I'm really too old now."

The woman then grew quiet and again gave Tommy a hard stare, as if trying to make out her features. She smacked her lips in frustration. "I wish I could see your face better."

"I'm sorry about that. I'm sorry you're blind."

"Yes, because I need to see your tattoo before I tell you anything more."

"Tattoo?"

"Yes. I just remembered that. Capri said if you were to come to see me that you'd have a tattoo. You probably think it's a birthmark, but Capri tattooed you. She told me that so that I would know you when you came. I just didn't know it would be this long of a time, and I'd get these damned cataracts, and that half my mind would be gone. Show me the thing."

"I . . ." Tommy stammered, thinking about her body art. She did have a couple of nice tats that she would be proud to show, but who knew where Capri had tattooed Romia? *What kind of mother tattoos a child, anyway!*

Tommy tried to think about the possibilities of just picking a random one, but being wrong could end everything, and she had not gotten enough information from this woman to take that chance.

"Your right ankle! Come on, show me. But then again, I can't see shit." The woman groaned. "Oh, I wish I could see it," the woman said.

Tommy sighed, relieved at the woman's frustrated blurting. "My ankle? I'm sorry. I'm in a boot. I was hurt and I'm in a boot now so it's covered up or I'd show you."

"I thought you sounded strange when you walked in. I have hardwood floors for that reason. One day I'll be totally blind and I'll need to rely on my senses. I'll need to be able to hear people walking and know who they are. Capri told me to always rely on my senses, that they were my greatest assets. I thought she was nuts back then but, damn, if that girl didn't know what she was talkin' about. I'm blind as a bat!"

"Yes, the senses are very important."

"You should know," the woman said, shaking her head. "Capri had very highly developed senses. That's how she knew so much about what was going to happen to her. She was truly amazing. Once you got past thinking she was a lunatic. She said one of her children had those kinds of gifts. Is it you?"

"Children? I . . . I'm not sure," Tommy said, trying not to show her surprise.

"Do you sense things like when something is going to happen? Do you have strange dreams that tell the future and stuff like that?" the woman asked, sounding excited.

"Um, I don't know. Am I supposed to?"

"Oh, yes, all of the Phoenixes are supposed to; they have to survive you know. 'They have to stay ahead of the enemy,' Capri would say," the woman said, confirming what Jim had read in the secret report. "Capri said that your father could do other things that were truly just too fantastic to even believe. She said he could walk through fire. I didn't believe that part but . . . So what do you do special?" she asked, changing the subject quickly.

"Without my mother, how am I supposed to know what I do special?"

The woman's face frowned up a little. "By now, you should know something. My God, your father is supposed to have been extraordinarily gifted, or so Capri said. She said by the time you grew up, all of you would be reunited and ruling the world—well, she didn't say that, but the way she described it, you'd think that's what she meant. Phoenix this and Phoenix that—yeah, let that girl tell it, you all were royalty in the spy business."

Tommy tried to imagine Romia with "gifts." Romia was strange. Maybe she did know what her gifts were, and maybe that's why she was so strange.

Fire walking, telekinetic paranormal freak; yeah, that would be Romi. Poor thing, Tommy thought, suddenly feeling the burden that would hinder a kid with "different" parents, like Romia apparently had. Like she needed people adding that to her resume of oddness. "I don't want to be different. Wait, you said spy," Tommy then blurted, realizing what the woman had said.

"Oh, shit," the woman spat, shaking her head again. "Well, hell, you probably know that already and are just pretending not to, but yeah. Your mother was a spy for government—or so she said." The woman left the room and came back with a small envelope. "Here is a letter from your mother. I've never opened it. It's for you. When she died, we packed her things, me and Mildred. Mildred died a while back so I have most of the stuff now, but this is the only real important thing Capri really wanted you to have. I've kept it safe all these years. Even without my sight, I always kept my eye on this baby."

Tommy took the letter and tucked it in her jacket. "Thank you. So you know for sure my mother's dead."

"Yes. They killed her. Just like she said they would. I suspect she put up a huge fight I mean, how do you kill a person like her?"

"What about my father?"

The woman frowned again. "Now, Romia, you know I don't know anything about him, and you should know better than to ask."

"But I thought you said my mother said we'd all reunite . . ."

The woman stood now and took a deep breath. She then smiled sadly. "I think you better go, young lady. If you really are Romia, they're looking for you, and I sure don't want them finding you here."

"Do you know who *they* are?"

"The enemies of the Phoenix, of course. You and your twin are chosen and the last of your kind . . . well, unless you procreate." She snickered. "But your poor mother saw what a mistake that was . . . no offense. So she hid the two of you in separate places so neither your father, grandfather or anybody could find you before it was time. Her dying messed it up, but that wasn't her fault. She was just an innocent girl who got involved with the wrong man."

"You're saying she'd still be alive if she hadn't had me, I mean, us?" Tommy asked, standing up.

The woman shrugged. "That's how I figure it. I mean, they'da just killed your father and ended it at that. But I'm just an old woman—what do I know . . ."

Chapter 37

Romia watched as the once-adversary-now-turned-comrade moved gracefully across the floor. His steps were as fluid as a ballet dancer's. His muscles twitched only slightly with each difficult movement; he was beautiful. She watched in awe, breathless and quiet as he, silently and without flaw, climbed the rope to the top of the rafters. He then quickly ran across the beam to the open window, through which he descended without a sound. Suddenly, and within only seconds, it seemed, he entered the bar door behind her. Creeping up to her quickly, he grabbed her tightly around the waist, lifting her from her feet. Before thinking, or reacting by defending the playful attack with a vicious response, which should have been her reaction, she found herself giggling.

Instead of fighting him, she gave into laughter, kicking her feet high over her head as he swung her around, making airplane sounds. Suddenly, she remembered that he too was the enemy. Not since they'd landed her in this strange place, and moved into this farmhouse in the countryside, had she one civil conversation with anyone about anything important or relevant to her life. "Stop, Royale. This isn't funny," she growled, unable to make her voice as menacing as she had hoped. It was unlike her to be this giddy, and she choked on the sound of her own mirth.

"I know. This is work," he retorted, letting her go at the high point of the swing. She yelped but landed on her feet like a cat, crouched and ready for the fight that came immediately.

Sparring with Royale was like fighting a mirror. He sensed her every move, as if reading her mind; sometimes attacking her with the move she had only in her mind planned for him. He struck her. Only now, instead of drawing blood, he lightly tapped her face. "Point!" he yelled out.

Growling, Romia's frustration grew and so did her speed. She began new combinations, ones she'd only just created within the moment.

His eyes widened and he backed away slightly, blocking awkwardly.

Finally, upon an opening, she tagged him with the heel of her foot to his chin. Royale fell backward in the hay. "Point," she purred, breathing heavily with her hands on her hips in a bragger stance.

Blindingly fast, Royale recovered, kicking her feet out from under her, sending her flying forward into his lap.

The moment was long, close, and increasingly comfortable, more comfortable than Romia would have ever imagined it to be. It was intimate, and demanding of a kiss. Their lips closed in.

Her brain forced her eyes to close, but before they shut, before she was left to only enjoy the sensation of his full mouth on hers, or more, "Get off me," Royale yelped, pushing her backward and jumping to his feet.

Romia, flustered and still a little confused by the moment, hesitated for an instant before moving her hair out of her face. "How do you do that?" she asked, immediately regaining the moment.

"What?" he asked, wiping his face with a handy towel. "Use a towel? It's easy, you just go like this." He covered his face with the towel again, scrubbing vigorously.

"No, stupid." Romia chuckled, shaking her head. "How do you move like that? Like me?"

Royale lowered the towel, catching her up in his gaze. "Your moves are not so unique."

"Yes, they are. I make them up as I do them. So how—"

"Well . . ." he said, allowing the sentence to hang while his green eyes sparkled like a pool of water, just as her mother's used to, only hers were pools of blue. His crooked smile was familiar and unnerving. She shook her head, turning away from what was now turning into a painful exchange. "Apparently they aren't," he answered, tossing the towel at her.

"Nasty! I don't want this. It's full of sweat! Your sweat!" she yelled, throwing it back and hopping to her feet. "I'm gonna go grab a shower, and, um, you should too. You smell really bad," she smarted off before playfully swinging on him one more time and walking past. He ducked her easily.

Walking toward the door, her hips swayed uncontrollably. She could feel them moving, but was unable to stop the movement. She knew he was watching, but she couldn't stop the flirtatious show her body insisted on performing. Without looking back at him, she headed out of the barn and back to the big house.

"Hey!" he called to her. She turned. "You ever wonder . . ." He paused. "You ever wonder what Maxwell is really up to?"

Romia's heart tightened along with her stomach. She had been fighting for weeks the doubt and lack of trust toward Maxwell Huntington, but now it all flooded back. "No," she lied. "He said he's trying to find my father, to help him. I have to believe it. Not every procedure is by the book I'm used to reading. The more I thought about it, the more I could see the possibilities of it being true, the things he says. You can't choose your parents, and maybe it was for my own good they cut me loose and let me grow up to be a cop."

"Aw," Royale responded, almost sounding disappointed. "Well, I do. I mean, I've been working with him for a long time. But still, sometimes I wonder."

"How long?"

"Well, since he . . ." Royale's eyes went to the sky as if contemplating a word. "Acquired me. Adopted me," he corrected.

"He's your father?" Romia asked.

Royale's head went back in laughter. "Well, no. I mean, yes. I mean, I was sixteen when he adopted me. It's not like I didn't know he is not my father."

"Where were you living?"

"I was in a convent in France. I lived there for as long as I remember. The nuns said my mother birthed me as a baby and ran off in the night."

"Well, birthing a *baby* would be how she did it all right." Romia chuckled, trying to lighten the moment. Royale always made her laugh, even when he wasn't intending to. She felt silly and carefree. It was unusual for her, yet easy to give into.

"Funny, *cherie*, but no, it's serious. I do not know my mother or my father. But Maxwell came and got me and he's been the only father I know. But . . ."

"But sometimes you doubt him?"

"And you never doubted your mother? It seems to me she was worth doubting."

"She died when I was young. Or at least I thought she did. She was wonderful and beautiful and . . ."

Royale grinned broadly, holding open the door for her to enter the large foyer. "And apparently someone worth doubting," Royale added. "So what do you think about your father being the Phoenix who everyone is looking for?"

"I don't want talk about this," Romia said, growing instantly uncomfortable.

Inside the house, there were no obvious indications of spy activity, but Romia was more than certain everything and everyone was under observation. Perhaps that was the normal way of spies: to be covert, even with each other. Or maybe Romia was just being paranoid. She'd never given much thought to underworld activity until now. Sometimes Keliegh would speculate about such things, sounding as obtuse as those who believed in life on other planets. Yet here she was, as if on the moon. If only he could see her now.

She was learning faster than she could ever imagine learning anything and even in just this short month she'd picked up many fighting skills and mesmerizing talents, along with a working knowledge of Arabic and French. Maxwell spoke Arabic all the time and, despite her inability to speak it back, she seemed to understand him well.

Royale?

It was if he'd been speaking to her his entire life. She always understood him and, lately, had been able to speak back to him in his native language, which amazed both of them.

In addition to fighting skills, Romia had become exposed to kinetics, the mind's natural ability to enhance rates of chemical reactions within the body. At first, these abilities appeared to be supernatural. When Romia witnessed Jerry—the undead man—and his ability to conduct electricity to the point of shorting out a fuse box, she was impressed. And then there was Royale and his telekinetic ability to move small objects with his mind, and his slightly inept pyrokinetic ability to start small fires. He claimed to be mastering the latter, but all Romia had seen was one mishap after the other.

The woman, Olga, turned out to be quite the talented one. She was an expert forger and voiceover whiz. She could emulate any female voice she heard more than once. "When did you have occasion to imitate Tommy like that?" Romia asked upon hearing her first impression. Olga just laughed sarcastically and then repeated Romia's words in her own voice. Romia knew not to ask any more of the strange woman. She was a master magician as well, rivaling David Copperfield and bordering on the abilities of Houdini. She was a queen at sleight of hand. Romia was eager to learn a few of those tricks, as she remembered her mother's ability with cards and coins.

Memories of her mother were slightly painful now, knowing the lies she'd lived. All the years living in that foster home, wondering why God had allowed her to be abandoned that way, only now to find out God had nothing to do with it.

Upon entering the house, Olga spoke to Royale in German. He answered in the same dialect, to which they both laughed. Romia hated not understanding all the foreign languages this group of people spoke. She distinguished at least three—Arabic, French, and German. She would have to speak with Maxwell about lessons in German next.

So far being here in the countryside of Buren had been grand. Although they were living quite covertly, they were living above suspicion. No one around them seemed concerned about their comings and goings, and Romia hadn't asked what their covers were.

In a way, it seemed rather entertaining to be spies. Everything bad that had happened last month seemed to have gone away, as if it had never occurred. Romia half expected to have the three goons from the tavern show up, explaining that incident too was part of the façade she was now living. But she knew in her heart that all of that was real. Mike was dead and she had committed murder, albeit in self-defense. She was a fugitive. She knew that. She knew she'd have to one day return to face justice.

Justice? Did she even know what that was anymore?

Chapter 38

About a year before, in Portsmouth, New Hampshire

Her dark eyes were wild and dancing. Her raven hair flew in the wind that her speed had created. He wasn't sure he knew her yet; there was something very familiar about her.

"Thank you for seeing me, Mr. Akimbo, on such short notice," she said, stepping forward to shake his hand. He stood from where he sat behind his desk. She stopped in her tracks before reaching his desk, just long enough for him to look deep into her eyes, long enough for him to recognize her behind those dark-colored contacts. She lunged forward, stopping her face from colliding into his by only inches.

"You're in danger," she said, sounding breathless, as if having flown in from wherever she was from. Her voice was low and she spoke in clear English, no accent.

"Who are you?"

She didn't smile, but continued to speak. "You need to hide. You must hide."

"I don't know what you're talking about." He reached for the phone, but she stopped him by placing her hand over his. He took note of her soft hand. Again their eyes met. He was mesmerized. Just gazing into them calmed his spirit. There was only one other woman on earth who had affected him this way. She was the only woman he ever loved.

"Capri?" he whispered.

She looked around and then back at him. "Yes, Malik."

"I thought you were dead."

"Too many times. I've been dead too many times. But always it has been my love for one of you that has brought me back."

"Your love?"

"Yes . . . and now I've come to warn you."

"Of what?"

"He's going to kill you."

"Me?"

"You, me . . . Stone."

"Stone? Stone is dead."

"He's not dead. Don't say that. Besides, if he were dead, we'd all be dead."

Malik pondered the truth to those words. Surely, Stone's nemesis and archrival would find them first, torture them, and gain access to Stone. But surely Stone, wherever he was, was undetectable at this point. *Why would he upset his cushy life by coming out in the open? He escaped the repercussion, of being the son of a mastermind like the Pheonix years ago and never looked back,* Malik thought, realizing then that he felt a little resentment. Even after all that had happened with his father's organization, Stone didn't show one ounce of care.

"I'm through with all the killing," Stone had said, spinning his *shot glass around between his palms.*

"But killing isn't through with you. It will always be in your blood."

"If I kill again, it will be for a purpose of my own making. It will be for a purpose I understand."

"If they find that you are alive, they will hunt you down. You can't run from your destiny."

"No one will ever find me, unless you expose me." Stone grabbed the front of his jacket as if he were about to tear him limb from limb.

Despite what had happened so many years ago that day in that hotel room, Stone had refused to accept betrayal from Malik.

The silence between them grew thick. Malik remembered the feel-

ing he felt at that moment. If Stone killed him, he'd in the afterlife haunt him forever or at least until he returned the favor, but if Stone let him live it would only prove their friendship now and forever.

Stone released his collar. "You are truly my brother," he said then.

Malik didn't answer. He didn't need to. Since finding out Stone had survived that day, Malik had kept this fact a secret. Perhaps the Phoenix knew, but if so, that secret died with him, as no one had found Stone and probably never would.

"I'm married," Stone said then.

Malik smiled. "Really?"

"Yes." Stone grinned and Malik could have sworn he saw a blush run across his cheeks.

"You love her more than anything."

"More than anything, or anyone."

"Anyone . . ."

"More than anyone," he repeated. Malik sensed then that Stone knew somehow about Capri sleeping with Stix.

Stix had tried to kill him many years ago and although he failed, he was unaware of that and moved on into Stone's life as if he had succeeded. He'd moved into Capri's bed and claimed what should have been Stone's as far as leadership in the family. Everyone in the loop alluded to the assumption that Stix had betrayed the Phoenix in order to curry favor with the government. The thought was that he had been captured, and in return for mercy, he gave up the hiding place of his gifted father and exceptionally enabled family, turning them over to science, torture, and other inhumane treatment in the quest for understanding the paranormal.

"We are not paranormal," Stone would tell them when some would question their place in the universe. "We are normal. We just use our minds in different ways. True, we are exploited but, in the end, we are housed, clothed, fed, and in a strange way . . . loved." It was true, the Phoenix did love them. He even loved Stix. It was Stix who had no love for them.

Malik wasn't sure if Stone knew about Capri's pregnancy, but

*either way he knew it was futile to try to convince him that the child
was not Stix's, especially knowing that the child's paternity had not
been officially determined. Yes, Capri had sworn to him that the
baby in her womb belonged to Stone and that Stix had forced her to
bed down with him, but in reality there was no way he could confirm
the truth, considering she continued to allow Stix to visit her bed.
Malik didn't even know for sure if Capri had given birth to the baby.
The last he had seen her, he dropped her at the convent, pregnant.
The next he heard, some six years later, was that she was dead.*

*Capri was a hard woman to trust. But now, she was dead—or so
he thought. So why even bring her up to Stone as he talked about his
new life? There was nothing left but to move on. It was much later he
found out she had not died. By then, he too, had moved on.*

*"That's wonderful, my friend," Malik had said, patting his shoul-
der. "Live long and prosper as they say."*

"The dead always do." Stone laughed.

Malik thought about that secret meeting from over twenty
years ago.

"The government has long been satisfied with the amount
of blood they've collected from our family. They have become
bored with us, Capri. They're tired of looking for Stone. The
Phoenix is dead. We're all dead. You should stay dead and get
a life," Malik said, sitting back in his chair now, breaking the
spell of her eyes.

Now he folded his hands across his chest to make sure they
were unavailable to her. He didn't want to chance her touching him again. It had been years since he'd seen her, but it was
as if it were yesterday with what he felt growing inside.

Love and hate. Capri made the line so thin.

After his meeting with Stone in Europe all those years ago,
he moved to the US. He'd moved to New Hampshire. At that
time, he still thought Capri was dead. He hadn't seen Stone
again, and Stix . . . Stix often crossed his mind. The thought
of Stix kept his life in motion. Maybe it was his personality,

but he couldn't live with the same calm that others apparently could. He had a heightened sense of the impending. He knew soon he'd have to allow that ability to die down if he were to ever have peace. For at that time it was forever with him. Back then, he was still uneasy about life in the US. Back then, he still feared for his life sometimes and all strangers made him leery. He was on the run and he'd not grown comfortable with his life.

Malik had just taken the position at the company where he stayed and now worked as a high-level manager in IT. Back then, he wasn't making the money he was making now. When he saw Capri that day, he couldn't believe his eyes at first, but then, with Capri, anything was possible. Was it happenstance running into her? No, he didn't believe it. For, with Capri, could anything really be an accident? All this time he had thought she was dead and now here she was.

Back then, there were so many things to ask her, to talk about. He took her to his apartment so that they could enjoy the reacquainting. Before he knew it they were making love. Amazing as it was, it was wrong. Malik, in his heart, knew it was wrong. Despite the fact that Stone had moved on, there was something illicit about having Capri in this way. Malik's concerns were confirmed when later, during dinner, she began to question him about Stone. She was digging for information. It was as if she was reading his mind and knew he had been in contact with Stone since the day they left him for dead.

She knew he was alive, Malik believed that. He realized then that Capri had used him—for comfort, for information, for whatever reason. She had used him and it wasn't for love. In his heart, he wondered now about her love affair with the two brothers.

What had been her true motives for coming between them the way she had?

"You have to contact Stone and tell him," she said then, bringing Malik's attention back to her presence in his office.

"I told you. He's dead."

"You lie, Malik. I know he is not dead."

"Then you find him. You tell him." At that Malik was on his feet and moving around the office. He was moving as if a target avoiding a spear. His heart, he was guarding his heart. He'd turned away from her, facing the window. "Why did you come here? If you are being followed, why on earth would you come here? Why would you lead them to me?"

"I didn't, Malik. They are not following me. I made sure of it. I would never do that to you. I just knew you were the only one I could trust. You know all my secrets. It takes us together to make it work. Why do you think we were always assigned to work together? It takes the two of us. You—"

"I do? I know all your secrets?" he asked without turning to her. "Then answer me this Capri—whose child did you give birth to? Stix's or Stone's? Tell me that."

"Both," she whispered.

He turned to see her expression but instead he only saw an empty office. She'd seemingly vanished. He walked out to where his secretary sat. She seemed undisturbed. He wondered if she'd even see her leave. He didn't even bother to ask. Maybe she'd never even been there.

"Both?" he mumbled under his breath.

"What? Mr. Akimbo, did you say something to me?" his secretary asked.

"No, no, I didn't . . . Uh, I'm leaving early."

Leaving the office after collecting himself, Malik was not at peace. He felt watched and uneasy. It had been years since he'd felt this way. Capri was right. It always took their abilities working together to finish the unforeseen. It always took Malik's ability to feel the jumbled pieces of the impending future and Capri's telekinetic abilities to put the pieces together.

Separated from her, Malik stayed consumed with anxiety most of the time. Even now he took anxiety medication to ease the feeling.

When the Phoenix was assassinated it was through channels of extreme discretion that the remaining few family members communicated with him and with each other. Despite his breaking off from the 'family' years earlier when he ran off with Capri, he'd kept in touch, especially after finding out that Stone was still alive. He never told anyone for fear of betrayal, but gathered information in case his friend needed the information for his safety. He knew he'd be able to channel in on him and find him if he needed to—if it meant saving his life.

Newspaper ads, junk mail, chance meetings in the marketplace where discussions of the weather held codes full of pertinent information. There was rumor that some had started working for the government, helping them to find those family members who had escaped. Soon no one trusted anyone anymore and living became a lonely endeavor.

As far as he knew back then, Capri was dead, Stix was gone, and the Phoenix was a just a page in the government's espionage history. Eventually, he accepted that he'd never see Stone again, either.

Soon Malik felt a lightening of his spirit. Maybe it was the medication for anxiety but he really began to believe that his troubles were over. The government had rounded up and turned out as many of the family as they could and none of their efforts produced Stone. They finally accepted that he was dead—or so it seemed. It never really occurred to him why he'd been left alone. There had never been an attempt to turn or capture him. No interrogation. Never once had he been pulled in by the government. He never thought about the possibilities of his life being under close surveillance. Not until today. Now with this revelation from Capri he needed to see his friend again. What Capri had said was fierce and could change their lives.

If they were again being sought by someone, they needed to know who and why.

"Why would she come to me like that?" he asked himself. "Why would she come from the ashes that way and trouble my spirit?" he said, not really noting his own words and references to the mythical Phoenix. "And asking about Stone of all people. Has she been turned?"

He reached his condo but sat in his car for a moment or two just staring at his front door, pondering the question. His home that had brought peace and sanctuary for some time now suddenly felt queer and unwelcoming. It felt invaded.

Finally, stepping from his car, he tossed his keys back and forth in his hands, causing them to jingle loudly. The noise seemed to fill an uncomfortable silence of his neighborhood.

His neighbors seemed vacant. No dogs barked. No children played. He looked around for some comfort but found none. Stepping on his porch, he slid the key into the doorknob but did not turn it. He paused. His senses sat on alert and for the first time in years, he felt the need to call upon his long abandoned skills. Stepping back off the porch, he moved into the yard. Looking around, he felt no one was watching. At his age, scaling the side of his condo without a ladder would surely draw attention, so he thought he'd just try to get into his house mentally instead of through the attic.

Focusing on the front window he envisioned his home, the contents, the feeling of everything in its place. The vision was disturbed by a foreboding. It was an unwelcome feeling, one of danger and death. He focused on it. With determination he sought out the exact location of the feeling. His mind moved through the living room. The door. The wire. The trigger. The five-minute timer set to now go off in less than one minute.

His eyes popped up.

"A bomb!" He gasped, rushing to his car and starting the engine. He had triggered it when sticking in the key. He had about a minute before it detonated.

Car alarms blasted on as sounds filled the once-quiet streets. Dogs barking. People screaming.

The explosion was enormous.

Chapter 39

Romia had been missing for three months now. The initial fire on her heels had cooled. Things seemed to be returning to normal for most of those on the department. The body of the man "killed" at The Spot suddenly appreared at the morgue after a "mix-up" with the files. He was identified as Sergeant Frank Boxler. The murder of Mike and the three Arab diplomats had been pinned on Romia as well. She was a fugitive from the law with the order to apprehend with due force, which Keliegh knew meant shoot first and ask questions later to many of his gun-happy colleagues like Hank and Aston. The thought of Romia being gunned down like a dog plagued Keliegh's peace, so in his spare time he searched for her.

He searched for answers, starting with an inquiry into the file of Frank Boxler—nothing. Mike—clean (after eliminating his past brushes with the law as inconsequential). The three Arab diplomats—sealed.

Keliegh knew that Tommy's injuries had also made it difficult for her to just put her mysterious colleague out of her mind, but he resisted asking her if she too had been digging around in the case. When together, the overt absence of the discussion of Romia was obvious, but putting Romia out of his mind was impossible.

"Who did you just call me?" Shashoni asked, pushing hard against his chest.

He looked down at her there underneath him, as her delightful writhing and wriggling had come to an abrupt stop. "What?" he panted.

"I said," she began, while squirming free from their coupling, "who did you just call me?"

As if a lightning bolt hit, he realized instantly whose name had slipped from his lips. "Shoni. I don't know what you're talking about," Keliegh lied.

Sitting upright in the bed, she covered her face dramatically before tossing her thick mane back and glaring at him with her big brown eyes wide. "You called me Romee. Romee and Shashoni don't sound that much alike. I do know my name when I hear it, by the way . . . anyway."

Flopping onto his back, Keliegh tried to think fast. His arm throbbed and his head ached. He thought about blaming his faux pas on his injuries, which were still fresh—in a way—but resisted. *Why make it worse?*

"Keliegh, you have to talk about this. If we are gonna be okay, you have to talk about this," she began. She loved inviting turmoil. Keliegh knew talking about Romia to Shashoni would fix nothing. She was a jealous woman. Even talking about Tommy brought out her crazy side.

"No, I don't. I don't need to talk about anything to anybody," he lied, pulling the covers off completely and climbing out of bed. He needed to talk to somebody and quick.

He walked into the kitchen and poured a tall glass of water, swallowing it down slowly. His mind was racing. It had been all day and that was probably why he'd said Romia's name. There were so many things that still didn't fit. He felt her presence again. She was close. She was closer than close—probably right under his nose.

The killings at the tavern. Why would she kill Mike? How did she kill Mike? I can understand the three Arabs—well, I can't, but . . .

People don't just snap and start killing people. Well, they do, but . . .

He took another swig. Just then his phone rang.

"Jack, it's Jim."

"Yeah," Keliegh answered Lawrence's partner, Jim Beem.

"I know it's late but can we talk?"

"About what?"

"I don't want to tell you over the phone."

"Fine, you wanna come over or—"

"No. Meet me at the Popeyes by the Cow Palace."

"Why there?"

"I'm hungry."

Hanging up the phone, Keliegh's stomach tightened. He knew Jim wanted to talk about Romia. She was in the air and it wasn't just his imagination. Jim had felt it too.

"Jim?" Keliegh asked aloud.

"Shashoni!" Shashoni snapped, standing in the hallway with her hand on her hips. "Not Jim. Not Romee," she said, exaggerating that name. "Shashoni, your girlfriend. Now come back to bed."

"Aw, Shashoni. Baby, look, I gotta go to work," he lied, rushing past her to the bathroom. He had time for a quick shower.

He had to grab a shower.

Shashoni followed him into the bathroom. "You are not leaving just like that. You are not gonna just wash us off and dash out the door just like that. We need to talk, Keliegh."

"No, no, we don't. By the way, what did happen to you that night?" he asked her.

"What night?" she answered, sounding confused.

"The night Romia supposedly shot that guy."

"I told you. I was drugged and driven around."

"No, you didn't. You never said you were drugged."

"Well, I was and—"

"Did you hear any conversation or—"

"No. I just remember all this noise. Like jabber like . . ."

"Like maybe another language like maybe Arabic?"

"I wouldn't know Arabic if I heard it," she said with a smirk and headed back toward the bedroom.

Keliegh knew they were through talking. It was always that way with Shashoni. She would invite conversation and then take it where she wanted it to go before ending it on her terms. Why he was still dealing with her was beyond him. He stepped into the waiting shower.

Chapter 40

"So what's got you still interested in this case?" Tommy asked Jim after he downed his cola and let out a large rude belch. She liked this guy, only God knew why. He was nothing like Keliegh. Jim was older, shorter, and white. Yet there was something "beatnik-kinda-cool" about this guy that heated her blood just a little bit.

"I'm a good detective and when I smell something that isn't as sweet as a . . ." He paused, as if rethinking a possible crude remark. "As I think it should smell, I look into it. The closer I looked at this, the less sense it started to make. It was huge and then just died out. That's like the first red flag."

"I agree. It was just too wild. I mean, it was like somebody wanted Romia out of the way or something. Romia was always strange, but a swerve? I'm just not convinced. I was never convinced so I did some snooping and—"

"You got a boyfriend?" Jim asked out of the blue.

Tommy hated this question. She shifted in her seat. He smiled and took a large bite of fried chicken leg. licked his finger, and then grinned crookedly. His jaw was filled with chicken. "I guess that's a no," he said.

"I wonder where Keliegh is," she said, looking around casually.

"Probably getting laid somewhere," Jim said, not noting her expression change.

She felt it change so she knew it did. Accepting that Keliegh didn't feel for her as she did for him was fine, but hearing it and being reminded of it bugged her.

"So, you wanna go out sometime?" Jim asked, taking a bite from the biscuit and then offering it to her to share.

She shook her head.

"Is that a no to the biscuit or to the date?"

"No, um, to the biscuit," she stammered.

"Tomorrow night then. A movie," Jim suggested.

He was a smooth one, she noticed. It made her smile thinking about how men liked to trap women into situations like this one. It was flattering as hell. Jim wasn't bad looking, either. Not at all. And it had been over a year since she'd had a date, one that had ended up where she knew Jim wanted theirs, too. She knew his reputation with the ladies.

And he's so short.

"Well, I . . ." she began, only to feel Keliegh's strong hands on the back of her neck as he slid into the seat next to her. Her eyes closed and when they opened they met Jim's. He just smiled and again took a long draw from his straw. Perhaps they had an understanding now. Who could tell?

"So, talk to me," Keliegh said, sounding casual and less than surprised that Tommy was there. "What have you two been up to . . . and without me. Shame on ya." He was joking, but Tommy still cleared her throat and felt her cheeks warm up.

"Yeah, about your ex, Romia—" Jim started out.

"She's not my ex," Keliegh blurted out.

He'd said it a little too quickly, in Tommy's opinion. She cleared her throat again. She was beyond uncomfortable now.

"Have you done any research on her mother and that supposed car accident?" Jim inquired, pushing his fries in Keliegh's direction. Keliegh quickly took a few before looking around toward the counter, as if suddenly realizing his hunger.

"No. Actually, I was more concerned about the current

events. Like those guys she killed at the tavern. Not the one she supposedly shot, 'cause that one gave me a headache, but the three big guys. The foreigners."

"Yeah, those guys freaked me out too, until I did a little research on Romia's mother. The car accident and then that she showed up again . . . shot."

"What? What are you talking about? Romia's mother? What is all this about her mother?" Keliegh asked, looking at both Jim and Tommy. It was clear that they had left him in the dark far too long. It had only been since last month that Jim and Tommy had conferred on the case. But both agreed they were getting nowhere fast and then it just sort of died. This was the first time since she'd told him she had visited the old woman that she really realized that Jim had still been at it. She had been too, so it worked out. But Keliegh they had left in the dark totally.

"Her mother was not American. Did you know that?"

"No," Keliegh said, sounding singsong and sarcastic while digging in his pocket for possible change for something to eat. "Like Americans are this hard to figure out . . ." He came out with a few bucks and stood up. "Of course she's not American. This case would have been just too easy." Jim nodded and Keliegh left the table for the counter.

Tommy always found male communication interesting. They were so non-verbal and primal . . . fascinating really. It was funny considering what she had to say was so much bigger than their trivia. Her research had yielded much more. She debated when to spring it on them. She'd told Jim she was going to check out some things but had yet to tell him what she'd found out a few weeks prior when she visited the old woman.

"So what nationality was she?" Keliegh asked, returning with a tented number to set on the table.

"French, as in from France," Jim answered.

"Really. So Romia is French?"

"Yeah. But we'd never know it from her birth certificate."

"Why is that?"

"It doesn't exist."

"Pardon? How did she get a driver's license and all that other stuff?" Keliegh asked.

"Well, legally she doesn't have one. Everything she has was gotten on an affidavit. As in 'we'll get it,' and whoever signed that never got it. And Romia, she's like a cash-and-carry chick. She's never done anything that really required her to show documentation."

"What about getting on the force?"

"I think by then her life had sorta been 'fixed.'"

"Fixed?"

"Fixed. Papers, identity, her life. It had been fixed. All her ducks had been put in a row by then."

Suddenly, both men running out of talk noticed Tommy's silence. "You said you did some investigating?" Jim asked.

Tommy cleared her throat. "Oh, yeah, and you're never gonna guess what I know."

"Then tell us so we don't have to."

Tommy reached into her satchel and pulled out the letter the old woman had given her.

Chapter 41

The three of them, Jim, Keliegh, and Tommy, read the letter, which led them to a report tucked away in the secret file. Jim used his connections to get it opened to them.

"She, uh, she and I, um, had dinner once," he awkwardly explained to Tommy, who just nodded.

"Umhmm . . . whatever, let's just see the file, shall we?" she said.

"Yeah," he mumbled, opening the file that was titled, "bizarre police cases, unresolved."

"Bunch of circus midgets and witch hunts." Jim balked, scanning a few of them quickly. Suddenly, their eyes ran across one of interest. "Wow, international—government clearance needed on this one," he said, pointing it out to Keliegh and Tommy, who read the query on the case. "This is like the one I got from the Bureau."

"You got into the Bureau files?" Keliegh asked, sounding both shocked and impressed.

"Another dinner?" Tommy asked. Jim blushed slightly.

"Wow, it's over thirty years they have been looking for these people," Keliegh said, ignoring Tommy and Jim's exchange.

"Yeah." Jim pointed at a dark-haired woman's picture associated with the file. "Look familiar?" This one showed the woman alive.

"Oh my God that's Romia!"

"No, it's not. This is over thirty years ago. Her name is Capri," Keliegh noticed.

"Has to be her mom then. What happened to her?"

"Ran over by a car over twenty years ago and then . . . and then shot . . ." Jim paused. "Two years ago. So who the hell knows where she is today."

The three looked at each other, allowing the words to sink in. "Romia's mother died twice?"

"Well, considering that scenario, you tell me."

"I wonder, does Romia know?"

"My guess is no, but somebody obviously thinks she does."

Tommy pulled the file closer and quickly glanced through some of the photos, tossing them aside for the written stuff. "What did she do for the government?"

"Doesn't say. Suffice it to be covert operations or we wouldn't need government clearance."

"We don't have government clearance," Tommy corrected.

"Yeah, that is true." Jim chuckled.

Just then, one of the male photos caught his eye. Keliegh picked it up and gave it a closer glance. "Hey, guys, he look familiar to you?"

At that, Tommy gasped.

Chapter 42

Romia was unable to sleep. Weeks had passed and things seemed to be headed nowhere. Aside from Maxwell's secretiveness and meetings in town, she wasn't sure at all what was going on. She felt like a member of a ring of thieves the way they all seemed to be just waiting around for the next victim. The only difference was their abilities. These people were not mere thieves; they were more than that. What they knew how to do could be very valuable in the right—or wrong—hands. Just then her door opened; it was Royale.

"I had locked the door."

"Locks mean very little to me," he chuckled. Moving close to the bed, he sat on it. She sat up, noticing his troubled face through the light coming in through the window.

"We are going to move soon. I can tell. Maxwell has had too many meetings in town and we are going to be moving soon."

"What is it you do when you move?" she asked.

He looked at her. "We go to work," he said.

"Work?"

He looked around as if knowing the walls had ears.

"You're okay with just doing as you are told, yes?" he asked.

"Well, do I have a choice?" she asked.

"You always have choices. Our parents had choices, we have choices."

"What do you know about your parents?" she asked him.

"I know my mother was a witch. At least, that's what the nuns say."

"That's awful for them to say that."

"No, I mean, what kind of mother carves her child with a knife days after he's born and—"

"She what?"

Clicking on the small lamp beside the bed, Royale propped his leg up on the dresser and raised his pant leg. Around his ankle was an ugly keloid. "See."

"I'm sorry," Romia sympathized. "Maybe she wanted to . . ." Romia thought about the implications of such an act by a mother. She knew her mother had put a small tattoo on her ankle but that was to always know her, or so she said. It was nothing so disfiguring as what was on Royale's ankle. Although it was a huge scar, it was ugly and oddly shaped. Using her imagination, she would say it was shaped somewhat like her tattoo, only raised above the skin as keloids commonly are.

"They say she read minds and had clairvoyant abilities," he went on, sharing with her thoughts on his mother.

"That still doesn't make her a witch. Many people have extrasensory perception. It's just how they use it."

Turning to the papers on her small dresser, he focused on them until smoke began to rise from them and eventually a small flame. He stamped it out with her slipper that lay on the floor. "A lot of people set fires, no?" Royale asked rhetorically.

"Well, Royale, that too is an anomaly, but not demonic. It's just an ability, sort of like Jerry and his electricity buildup, or me and the way I can open anything locked," she said. She got out of bed and walked over to the door. She turned the lock and showed him that it was locked by the twisted knob. She then closed herself outside the door. Turning the knob again, she walked in. "Locks mean very little to me as well."

"Wow," he said. "That could be useful for Maxwell. He

seems to like people with 'ability,'" he added. "He's been com-
plaining how few you showed."

"Yeah, well." She smirked, moving back over to her bed.
"I'm not a circus performer. There is a lot I know how to do
that he doesn't need to know about."

"You don't like him much, no?"

"I'm not sure what Maxwell is up to and I don't like that.
I'm not sure I want to do what he wants me to do. I'm not
sure I want to hunt down people for him."

"*Cherie*," Royale said, looking around. He pointed at the
light and then at the window.

Together they slipped through the open window and climbed silently onto the roof, closing the window behind them.
"I just feel . . ." she whispered. He put his finger to her lips.

"Since the first time I kicked your ass," Royale began. He
sounded tongue-in-cheek, and all Romia could do was smile.
"I felt a connection to you. Maybe it's love, I don't know. I
don't want to kiss you, or make love to you, so the feeling
confuses me. I know you love someone and I could never take
his place, nor do I want to, but, *cherie*, you and I, we are soul
mates, of this I am certain. My loyalties are with you. Just say
what you want to do and I will do it."

"What about Maxwell?"

"Maxwell has been like a father to me, this is true. But he
is not my father, and I have dreamed about such a man for a
long time, but I . . . I have been with Maxwell for many years,
hunting for men, killing them or betraying them for the government. I am trapped to him as a son. I don't like the life
and I want out."

"You will help me find my father and I will help you find
yours."

"It is not my father I seek, it is my mother. It burns at my
soul not knowing who she is."

"Then I'll help you find her."

"I think this is why we have been brought together in this space in time."

"Maxwell claims the people we are going to find need to be brought to justice. I don't believe it."

"I don't either. I've seen him kill," Royale confessed now. He looked off. "I have seen him kill not for the government, but for himself. I killed for him."

Romia touched his arm. He stared at her hand and then into her eyes. "I think I have too and I think he will have me kill again and . . ." She paused. "If I kill again, it will be for me."

"Then we will leave here."

"No. I have to end things in America. I agree with Maxwell. I have to end things there before I can move on."

Royale seemed to notice her sadness. "And the man Keleigh Jack?"

"I will love him forever," Romia admitted for the first time.

Chapter 43

Capri

French born, Capri had been trained to dance ballet before, at the young age of thirteen, she and her parents were involved in a horrible boating accident where she alone survived. Unable to live with relatives, she was moved to an orphanage, at a convent, where she thought all hopes and dreams of her happiness were lost.

She spent most of her time by herself, thinking, pondering, and visiting the voices in her mind for comfort. She would visit with her mother and father often in her mind, finding peace with their memory. Soon the voices became powerful to the point of angst to her soul. The voices were connected to people she wished she knew personally, for she hurt when they hurt and cried when they cried. One day, a tall, handsome, rich man and his wife visited the convent. They appeared to be lonely and looking for a child, at least, that was what Capri felt when the man brushed passed her. He said he wanted a son, yet, when they made that brief contact, Capri felt a pull from his spirit. He must have felt it too, as he turned around and looked at her. When their eyes met, one of the voices in Capri's head sounded out loudly.

"I know you," she said to the man.

"What?" the man answered.

One of the nuns ran over to hush Capri's apparent ramblings. "She's got a little of the darkness in her. We work with her constantly. She may have been born that way, or else it happened when she lost her parents. But she sees visions and talks to herself."

"What kind of visions?" the man asked.

"I don't see visions," Capri denied rebelliously. "I only see what you see," she admitted.

"And what do I see?" the man asked, squatting down to her eye level.

Capri touched his hand and closed her eyes. Instantly, they shot open and she stared deep into his steel grey orbs. The man smiled as if he knew his own darkness had frightened her, as if he knew she could not comprehend all the turmoil inside him. "I . . . I," she hesitated, dropping his hand and rubbing hers together and along the sides of her dress, as if they were hot and uncomfortable to her. "I didn't see any-thing," she lied.

That day, the tall, handsome, rich man and his wife took her home with them. He came to be known to her only as the Phoenix.

The man was Egyptian, not French, as she'd thought that day at the convent. He spoke many languages perfectly, in-cluding French, but the main was Arabic. His lovely wife was kind but it didn't take long before she seemed to fade away and another woman replaced her by his side. Then another, until she lost count and just accepted the women for who they were for the time they were. But the man was constant. He continued to treat her like a daughter of sorts, but then again, not. Capri got to dance sometimes with the other girls who lived there, and they all had fun and laughed. They too had been rescued from the grips of poverty, street life, and/or orphanages. They too saw visions, and some had even darker abilities.

The man was beyond attentive, making sure Capri had more than any girl could want. In return, she worked hard.

She learned many languages, skills of self-defense, and marksmanship, at which she excelled. She was obedient and attentive, especially when learning the art of internal examination: extreme self-control over her extrasensory perception, better known as ESP. She became one with her mind and gained the ability to control many things, much the way a telekinetic person would, only she was unable to move things. She honed her intuition and ability to decipher dreams to the point where she was depended on to foresee the short-term future. Before long, and after meeting Malik, who was clearly telekinetic, she learned that she too could move things with her mind. Together they worked toward that end. They became fast friends.

Having these abilities was frightening to her at first. Usually, she only opened doors or unlocked things, which eventually came in handy . . . especially when she realized her attraction for Stone.

Her attraction for Stone was the biggest event that she failed to foresee, and falling in love with him was something her extrasensory perception did not pick up on. It just happened. Had she foreseen this and what was to come beyond it, she would have fought the urges harder when they hit.

Stone was powerful, even for the young boy he was. He was more aggressive than the other boys. And, despite the admonition by the Phoenix to treat each other as siblings, by the time they were seventeen, she and Stone were having sex.

Sneaking off to the meadow, they would bask in the tall grass, under the sun and the warm winds, tanning their naked bodies on the blankets while exploring all the ways to please each other physically.

By the time they were nineteen, they were old lovers. There were one in spirit and soul, with Capri having the ability to read his thoughts and interpret his tumultuous dreams without even the need to touch him. It was his eyes that she read. They spoke volumes to her.

Stone had a troubled spirit, which often translated into high libido and hunger for her. They no longer took precautions when making love, as Stone would want sex any time of day or place without embarrassment. And she, hungry for him as well, would allow him to take her body without care or hesitation.

She realized she was pregnant two weeks after he died. She wasn't sure how to tell the Phoenix, but it became almost a moot point the night Stix came to her room. They hadn't spoken much about that day since but he felt the need tonight to talk to her, to set her straight on what she and Malik thought about his actions that day. But talking was the last of the things they did.

"You will love me," he said, as if now wanting to claim her as he had the team. He hovered over her in bed, pinning her to the mattress. He wasn't hurting her, as Stone was often rougher in his foreplay. But he wasn't Stone and she wanted him off of her.

"How can I love you?" she argued, attempting to pulled down her gown. He fought her for her dignity and what was not his—her body.

"You loved my brother. We are one, you know, he and I. You loved him, you can love me."

"We are all brothers and sisters here," Capri said, continuing her attempt to keep him from entering her body with his.

"No, we are not. You and I are not. We share no blood. Not like Stone and I," he explained, forcing her knees apart. "We are twins of separate mothers, both giving birth on the same night. We share a father; the Phoenix," he said, as if the mere sound of his father's name tasted bitter in his mouth.

Upon hearing it, Capri could not fight the bond that instantly was created between her and Stix. She searched his eyes for Stone. He was there. Until that moment, she did not know the truth about Stix and Stone's true bond.

Stix took her that night, claiming her as a conquest, and her impregnation as his own, once realizing she was with child.

The Phoenix was furious and refused to listen to the truth about whose baby she carried. He accused her again of betrayal and loyalty to Stix over Stone.

Malik helped her run away. Why, she never asked. She just took the offer and together they ran from the reach of the Phoenix, who she felt no longer trusted her and Stix.

Stix had become a tyrant in Stone's absence. Determined to be the leader, Stix had become insubordinate and downright subversive. He was at the root of two more siblings losing their lives on an assignment. His jealousy was apparent, and if he could not win the Phoenix's affections away from Stone's memory, he would destroy all that Stone had built. Why he hadn't been banished was a wonder to them all.

There was no way she wanted him to see the truth when she delivered Stone's baby. When Stone's spirit and soul poured out of her body on the face of his child, she knew Stix's jealousy would eat him alive. She feared he would kill the baby.

"You'll be safe here at the convent," Malik assured her that night, as he dropped her at the doorstep of her sanctuary, the convent where she was found. How poetic to return there. Malik fought back tears with all his might. Since Stone's death he'd been easy to bring to tears, and perhaps that was why he had chosen to leave with her. He was a deep soul, Malik. He felt things that he didn't share with her, and she felt in her heart they were feelings concerning Stone.

Where Malik once had the stomach for killing, he'd lost his edge, and maybe feared losing this life under Stix's careless renegade command if he stayed in the fold.

"I know I will be," Capri assured him. "I have Stone's spirit inside. He's always a part of me," she told him. "He will always be a part of you," she said, touching his face gently. "Thank you for believing me."

"I know you loved him. I saw it in your eyes."

"Yes. He will live forever now."

"The Phoenix will live forever. I thought you knew that."

"Yes, I do. I am to be damned for the part I play in that fact," Capri quickly interjected.

Malik seemed to understand and said nothing. He simply kissed both her cheeks and left in the night, thinking he would never been seen again.

She found peace there with the nuns for the remainder of her time. She felt safe and secure. It wasn't until the nights the pains hit that she grew fearful. She dreamed of Stone and felt his spirit close by. He was alive. She felt it. She sensed his presence. But his presence wasn't alone. It was joined by that of Stix.

The two spirits fought to the death. Before she could see the victor, she gave birth.

The nuns helped her during her labor. She thought she would die producing the two babies that wrestled in her womb: a boy and girl.

The boy came out of her big and red, as if on fire, and crying loudly. Surely he was filled with Stone's spirit. The girl was quiet, small, and sullen. She was dark in her heart. Stix had made his mark on her. Capri felt it in her bones that a miracle had occurred here. She had the souls of two brothers within her body and now within her heart. There was Stone, through the boy, and Stix, through the girl.

Capri knew immediately that she would have to take Stix's child with her so as to always know where Stix was. She couldn't have him sneaking up on her. She would leave Stone's child with the nuns for safety.

The boy screamed loudly when she carved the tiny wing of the Phoenix in his ankle. The girl, on the other hand, didn't make a sound when she did the same to her. Crossing their blood, she bound them together forever.

It was during the night she wrapped up her daughter in a blanket and left the convent undetected.

She knew the children would find each other one day, and all she could hope was that the spirits of their fathers would not destroy them first.

Chapter 44

"Before we can move forward on our task, we have to close up shop in America—with you," Maxwell said, pointing at Romia over the dinner table. They always ate together.

She looked around as if there were another Romia standing behind her chair. "Me?"

"Yes. Tomorrow we fly back and you will die," he said.

Romia's eyes widened and her muscles tensed. She felt Royale's hand land lightly on her shoulder. "Die?"

"It's okay, Romia, he doesn't mean it like it sounds. We've all had to do it," Royale said softly.

"It's not an actual death. It's signing off the books, so to speak. Your mother did it, your father did it, and all the members of the Phoenix team have done it, which is why they have been so hard to locate."

"So you're looking for members of the Phoenix team, of which I am not a part, so why must I do as they do?" she asked, considering how fresh her conversation with Royale about Maxwell's motives had been.

As if he felt his thoughts violated, he glared at her. "I never said or implied that."

"But, you said . . ." Romia began, before again feeling Royale's hand on her shoulder.

"We'll pack," Royale interjected.

Maxwell looked at the two of them strangely. "We?"

"Yes." Royale smiled.

Maxwell frowned. "She's a big girl, I'm sure she can pack

herself," he said, showing a sneer. "Besides, you two have been spending way too much time together."

"I suspect they are fucking," Olga said, to which Jerry chortled. Romia's face burned with embarrassment.

"You are simply jealous, no?" Royale asked Olga, allowing a wicked grin to cross his face.

"To hell with you! To burning hell!" Olga yelled, tossing her wine in his face.

Wiping his face dry with the napkin, he came back quickly. "I can stand the heat, can you?"

"You are a little boy in big men's clothes," Jerry said, attempting to join the argument, his Russian accent strong and husky. Romia watched Olga's, eyes. She was filled with rage, spit and all the other bad things a jealous woman feels.

"This little whore is nothing but trouble. From the start, she's been nothing but trouble," Olga blurted.

"Look, we can talk outside," Romia said then, sliding back her chair, ready to go a couple of rounds with her.

"Enough," Maxwell said.

Romia scooted back up to the table.

"Romia, you'll pack,"—Maxwell glared at Royale—"alone. Royale, we need to talk."

He jumped slightly as a thud was heard under the table. Olga had kicked him. She then buckled her lip and shook her head ever so slightly.

Romia realized then that the two of them had a secret.

Chapter 45

Yesterday

"Mr. Jackson, you have a call on line one."

"Thank you."

"What is it?"

"I hate to spring this on you but we're at red."

"Red? What happened to green and yellow, oh, and orange, and all those other pretty colors?"

"Stop your joking, you're always joking."

"My friends used to say the same thing."

"I can't imagine you having any friends."

"Yeah, well, there are a lot of things about me you probably couldn't imagine, but they're true."

"I'm sure they are. But back to business. I need you in Holland."

"Why?"

"We picked up a signal. If you get there right now you can catch him."

"I told you, catching him isn't enough. Besides, my kid has a recital tonight. I'm not going anywhere."

"Look here, Stone—"

"What did I tell you about calling me that!"

"Okay, okay, keep your shorts on, I'm sorry. It's just that we've been after this guy for a long-ass time, and, well . . ."

"I told you, when the time is right, I'll do it. He's not close enough yet."

"What? You want him in your living room?"

"Basically, yeah."

"You've made this way too personal."

"You're kidding me, right?"

There was a long silence on the other end of the phone. "Yeah . . . what am I thinking? I'm sorry. I know this is way over my head. I'm just following orders. I was told to call you and tell you we found the guy."

"Well, you did your job perfectly, Smithy. No worries. Now I'll do mine and we'll all sleep better knowing that I got a handle on the Phoenix situation."

Smithy chuckled nervously. "I will always think it's strange that . . . I don't know how to say this, but . . . that you're the one on this case."

"Why?"

"Well, hell, because of who are you are."

"And who am I, Smithy?" Bozman Jackson teased.

Smithy could be heard smacking his lips. It was as if he was scared to say the words, as if he knew the rules and played to them closely. Bozman Jackson was not the calm-spirited older gentleman he appeared to be. He was cold, ruthless, and worse, dangerous. Could he be trusted? No one was sure. But he was the man for this job and those orders had come directly from The White House. But Smithy knew too that those orders had an addendum: "one false move and Jackson was to be brought down by any means available." Smithy could only hope that would never happen on his watch.

"Have a good afternoon, Mr. Jackson," Smithy said, ending their conversation.

Chapter 46

The flight was long and tiring, but Romia couldn't rest. The thought of faking her death was frightening. What Maxwell wanted was a circus act. She was to allow Royale and his underdeveloped pyrokinetic abilities to start a distracting fire. This fire was to precede an explosion. She would avoid gunplay by hiding herself amid the explosion, and later be assumed burned. She didn't even want to know where Maxwell was going to find a female body that matched hers. The more she thought about his tactics for getting the job done, the less she trusted him.

He claimed over and over to be one of the good guys, but it just didn't seem that way. She and Royale had worked it out in their minds. They had connected the dots. There were too many references that just didn't add up. Maxwell just knew too many details about the inner workings of the Phoenix team.

"Either he was booted out, or he became a turncoat. That's how I see it," Romia told Royale as they walked through the market, picking out produce.

"Turncoat? This mean betrayal, yes?"

"Yes. I'm seeing this . . . I know he's not really Maxwell What's-His-Name, right? Well, have you ever wondered who he really is?"

"No," Royale said, tossing up a grape and catching it in his mouth.

"Can you be serious for a minute?"

"You are far too serious."

"Perhaps that's true, but"—she took a grape from his hand-basket, tossed it up, and caught it in her mouth—"I want to be on the right side."

"Which side is that?"

"The side that doesn't end up with me dead . . . really dead."

"I dig you," he said, causing her to burst into laughter. "You see? You can laugh and it's beautiful. I saw a picture of my mother once. The nuns had one. You look like her. She was beautiful too." He touched her hair. "She was amazing."

"You don't even know that."

"I can dream, can't I? If you think about it, she had more than one man in love with her. One was the father of her babies, the other a mad lover who caused her to run away in the night, another was one who brought her to safety. She was amazing."

"Babies . . ."

"I didn't tell you. Yes, I was so ugly and evil that she left me and took my sister."

Romia stopped walking and stared at him. He grinned at her before cocking his head to the side in question of her actions. "What was her name?"

"I don't know. You think they would tell me? No," he answered. "Those damned nuns," he fussed on. Romia chuckled, allowing her first wild thought to leave her mind.

"Yes, because you were so ugly and evil," she jeered.

He turned to walk backward. "Sticks and stones may break my bones but you will never hurt me," he said, grinning like a prince in a fairy tale.

Yes, it was her bones she was concerned about now, for Maxwell was nothing more than a sophisticated kidnapper. She thought about the cases where those kidnapped by cult groups eventually fell for the lies told by the leaders. Once they committed crimes on their behalves they were sold up the river by those leaders who allowed justice to be played out unjustly. *Not here, buddy. You'll go down long before I will. I want the truth and I'm going to find it. If my father is alive I'm going to find him. And if he's a criminal I'm going to do what I must, but it won't be based on your measure of what justice is.* Before anything went down in the US, Romia planned to do a little investigating on the Phoenix, now that she had more information to work with. Maxwell didn't know who he was fooling with.

He might just be in for the unexpected, Romia thought.

"You ready to die?" Maxwell asked her as if reading her thoughts, bringing her mentally back to the plane.

She looked over at him and shook her head, smiling weakly. "Are you?"

"*Touché,*" he said, reopening his magazine and flipping the pages.

Chapter 47

Tommy jolted awake. The banging on her door was relentless. She slid from under the sheet and grabbed her robe. Walking without the boot had her still favoring that ankle. Peeking through the blinds, she saw Keliegh's car, and groaned. She glanced at the clock. "Four A.M.? What the hell does he want?" she grumbled, shuffling to the door.

Before she could completely unchain it, he burst in.

"Oh my God. I'm being haunted."

"What?"

"Last night. Romia came to me. She was . . . she was a ghost. She must be dead or maybe it was a premonition but . . . oh my God," he stammered. He seemed in shock so Tommy tried not to laugh at his crazy hair and wild eyes. He was barefoot, and in his T-shirt and pajama pants as if he'd just jumped out of bed. Brushing past her, he ran to her kitchen and poured a cup of water, gulping it down.

"Slow down and tell me what happened," she asked, still trying to stay calm.

"It was Romia. I was asleep. But she woke me up. She was"—his eyes widened—"naked. God, she was beautiful. She, um . . ." He gulped, apparently noticing Tommy's blank expression. "She climbed on me and, well . . ." He chuckled then. "We did it. I mean, we didn't just do it, I mean, we . . ." He chuckled again. "We really did it, and then she told me not to worry about anything, that she was gonna be fine. She said she was with her kind and she was happy. And she laughed."

"Romia laughed?" Tommy asked. "I mean, like, ha ha ha?"

"Yeah, like she'd heard a big ol' joke. I asked her what she meant, you know, that comment . . . her kind, and that was all I could remember until like twenty minutes ago when I woke up and . . . and I came over here. I think she's dead and in heaven or something or I mean, if you'd seen her you'd know she was a angel for sure. I mean . . ."

Just then, Jim appeared in the hallway. Keliegh stopped speaking. He then noticed Tommy in her robe with clearly nothing underneath. Jim was without a shirt and only in his slacks that were no doubt leftover from his date attire the night before.

Keliegh, after allowing the shock to wear off his face, offered Jim dabs, which he accepted.

"Did she say anything about being with the Phoenix or anything like that?" Jim asked then, yawning and scratching his head, attempting to shake off the sleep.

Tommy rolled her eyes before stomping toward the bathroom. "Guys do we ever stop working?"

Chapter 48

The plan was simple. She was to come into the open and be seen. That was all that was needed, and Maxwell would do the rest. She had to trust him. He had information about her mother as well as her father that she needed. He was dangling a carrot in front of her.

Maybe he had the same information for Royale, who was out of sight right now, but clearly somewhere around. He was always around. It was strange how he, too, seemed to have the ability to disappear right in front of her. He puzzled her, and lately she'd been puzzling herself.

Watching him start small fires with just his mental control was frightening at first. He had told her he first developed the ability when he was around thirteen. The nuns at the convent found his ability to be disconcerting considering their beliefs of its origin. Apparently, the news of the firestarter spread in that small village until, finally, one day, Maxwell showed up and took him away from the convent.

"Acceptance is a powerful pull. Maxwell accepted me for who I am and what I am. For that I am to be forever grateful to him," Royale confessed. *"But that gratitude has separated itself from trust. I have you to thank for that."*

"Hey, it's Romia!" she heard an on-duty cop call out before calling in his sighting over the small radio.

She wore her jacket and her helmet, and rode through the streets in front of the precinct on her motorcycle before parking in front of the stationhouse. She worried about the possibilities of a sniper's bullet but she was sure Royale, Maxwell, Jerry, and Olga had that covered. They had a vested interest in her survival today. For what reasons, it didn't matter.

Within seconds the officers poured from the stationhouse, some with murder in their eyes, others with a little fear. She wasn't sure what stories they had heard, what Maxwell had planted in their minds about her, but none of it could make her feel any less accepted than she already felt.

Guns were drawn. Romia felt her chest tighten. She held out her arms. "I'm unarmed," she yelled out.

"Doesn't matter, Romia, and you know that," the captain said. He had come down from his tower to witness this. Romia knew then, this was huge. "Now, I'm gonna read you your rights. You're under arrest for the murder of Officer Frank Boxler, Mike Johnson, Akmir Tosiff, Enuabuli uh . . ." The captain was stumbling on the foreign names. "Zane Danzali, as well as acts of treason and terrorism against the United States of America."

Romia looked around for Maxwell. When did she become a terrorist? That wasn't part of the plan. Her emotions grew. Her lips tightened. This wasn't part of the plan.

"You will be tried in a court of law," the captain continued to call out. "Anything you say can and will be used against you," he said before fanning his hand to two officers who were assigned to put the cuffs on her. As they stepped forward she stepped back. She felt in the open and exposed. She no longer felt trusting that she had backup. Maybe she was just used to the way her fellow officers did it. Like now they crowded the streets, ready to take her down.

"Romia, don't run," the officer said, holding out his cuffs and stepping toward her as if she were an animal—one that bit or struck quickly like a snake.

Her emotions grew. In her hand she held a small signaling

device. With it she would signal Royale when it was time for him to act. She scanned the crowd for his face, but did not see him. Suddenly, a small fire broke out from behind the crowd. She couldn't help but smile. He'd done his best, but still his abilities were underdeveloped. She had watched him for weeks starting small fires, but did not want to tell him that she too had tried it and started a fire she could almost not contain. The memory made her chuckle.

Up her sleeve also, she concealed an incendiary device that, ignited, would send a flame at least twenty feet. She hadn't told Maxwell she had strapped it on, but she had planned to use it in case of emergency. In case her thoughts on him were right and he was going to betray her this day.

The plan was working so far, however, and the men were divided now, some tending to the fire, some still focused on her. "Step back," she warned.

"Come on, Romia, don't make this hard."

Suddenly Keliegh called out, "Romia!"

Another fire, slightly bigger, popped up; this one came with a few sparks, as if maybe Royale had used a device much like what she had up her sleeve.

A gunshot twanged as if ricocheting off a building. Chaos now ensued.

Distraction overtook her as she looked away from the officer toward Keliegh's voice. At that, an officer grabbed one of her her outstretched arms. She threw him off with a hard side kick and again swept the crowd for Keliegh. He appeared, just as a second officer came at her with a stun gun. He didn't make it far. She wasn't going to let him get close with that weapon. He hit the ground hard, with the help of her foot.

"Keliegh!" she called out, headed toward him.

Another office grabbed him, pulling him toward the ruckus. He fought him but was pulled into the crowd that seemed to grow bigger with each second.

The officer lunged at her, only to receive a work over from her quick hands. She was angry instantly. The officer looked up at her from where he lay on the ground. Her glare caused him to shake his head in apparent surrender.

"Fine, Romia, fine," he said, coughing out blood.

"Keliegh," she called out, pulling off the helmet. She wore it only to protect her hair if in fact she had to set herself on fire or in case Royale missed his target and set her on fire instead.

Spying Keliegh, he turned to her. Their eyes locked. Inside she knew then that they had connected in their souls. Her heart melted at the sight of his smile. He loved her. She knew it.

Starting toward her, he was stopped by the captain coming between them. "Keliegh you'll lose your badge this time," he threatened.

Suddenly she felt the tug of someone grabbing her arms and locking the cuffs on her wrists.

She kicked backward, landing the kick in the officer's groin. Swinging the helmet at him, she batted his head. He crumpled on the ground.

"Romia," Keliegh yelled, breaking past the captain.

She couldn't let him risk his career. It was all he had.

Olga had taught her this magic trick, and it was easy to slide the locked cuff from her wrist and toss it to the side. She could see the captain's eyes widen. "Stay away from me, Keleigh," she screamed, hoping to sound convincing that she really didn't want him to hold her, kiss her, and take her away from all this madness.

Fire trucks roared onto the scene. It was a madhouse now with neighboring residents in the street wondering what all the uproar in this normally quiet neighborhood was.

"Romia! You're . . . you're . . . a witch," the captain exclaimed. Yes, they had been fed much propaganda she could tell.

Suddenly, an explosion erupted within the stationhouse. Royale was feeling his oats now she thought. Everyone's attention was turned to this new fire. She slammed the helmet back on her head.

"Romia, stop it. I don't know what's going on with you and why you've gone to the dark side but stop it right now!" the captain barked.

Romia lips turned into a wicked smile. If only they understood magic with this smoke and mirrors they would have known the truth. But no, they wanted to believe she was a witch, and as she had always thought to herself, *If I were a witch, you'd never catch me to prove it!*

Within seconds she raised her arms. "I am the Phoenix," she said, admitting what she had only pondered from Maxwell's story regarding her parents—her father.

Any good detective had done the research by now, and Keliegh was a good detective. Her announcement clearly had not surprised him. She pushed the button on the device that would set off the fire that was designed to ride the top of her specially designed clothing. The way it's done in the movies. She had thirty seconds now to escape.

Aiming the incendiary device toward her bike, she shot the flames. She would miss her friend (her bike) but it was time they parted. The bike exploded as it was loaded with explosives designed for a full fireworks display, just like the movies. There were louder yelps from the crowd as some were taken off their feet by the power of the blast. She could see Keliegh's eyes through the glass of the helmet. He stood his ground as she turned and walked toward the flames. He called to her to stop but not before another explosion reverberated. This one came from a fire truck that apparently was parked too close to the bike. It was too close to Keliegh, too.

He was down.

Her first instinct was to stop and help him, but she couldn't. She had ten seconds to get to safety. At that instant, Royale appeared on the other side of the flames. He was singed but smiling, dressed in a police uniform, which he stripped away like a dancer on the Chippendale stage.

No one seemed to care about what they were doing now. No one seemed to comprehend that they were about to make their escape.

Human nature was truly amazing. What was expected was what occurred. The rest was for Maxwell to handle and Romia didn't care how he did it. She had done her part and given them the belief that she had taken her own life by walking into the flames.

Now she and Royale would get back to their plan.

Leaving a single life to live a double one was an odd fact to focus on at the moment so she tried not to. After quickly ripping the charred leather from her body and tossing the helmet aside, she and Royale climbed on his waiting motorcycle.

Slamming the helmets on their heads, they appeared to be young beatniks out for a warm day in the city: he in his black tee and black skinny jeans with trooper boots, and she wearing the female version of the same. No one paid them any extra attention amid the crazy scene playing out in the streets.

Chapter 49

One week later

Keliegh lay in the hospital bed. It was more than obvious that he was hurt worse than she could have first imagined. Her heart tightened. She wanted to touch him, hold him, to beg him to forgive her. But no, she had to only watch him lay there, helpless. Maybe he wasn't in pain. Perhaps the burns would not scar his beauty. It was the best she could hope for. His face was peaceful, soft, and despite the obvious cuts and bruises, still as handsome as ever. She would only imagine his soulful brown eyes as they were closed in deep sleep.

"I'm sorry, Keliegh," she whispered after making her way closer to his bedside. "I'm sorry I'm who I am and must do what I must do. It's a bigger calling than this life I've been living. It's so big. It's . . ." Romia shook her head. "I have to find my father. I have to help him bring Maxwell down. I didn't know at first but I know now and . . ." She shook her head, feeling the confusion coming on again, the tug at her ethics. Her entire life had been a lie. Her training in martial arts, her life in the foster home, all a ploy and plot designed by her mother for this day. Surely her mother knew this day would come and maybe she had hoped to join her in this mission— side by side as avengers of justice.

Again she shook her head as if questioning the justice that Maxwell Huntington claimed needing to be avenged. He was a liar and a fraud. He was the bad guy. It hadn't taken too many hours to find out the truth about the Phoenix team.

Maxwell's story changed so often she had no more trust for him and no choice but to do the research on her own. He was a fishy character from the start, and there was no doubt in her mind his claims of helping her after those men tried to kill her were selfish. For all she knew, he'd set her up; hell, he'd done it with Jerry and Olga. He'd ruined her career and, dare she say, her life. He needed to pay for that one just on GP.

But now to realize that he could have been behind the murder of her mother was too much. "And this dance, this Sherlock-Moriarty dance that he's doing with my father . . . I have to be a part of this ending," she said to Keliegh as he lay there, not hearing her.

"Why he is so obsessed with trying to destroy the Phoenix team, I don't know. Heck, I don't even know what side of the law the Phoenix team is on. Maybe we're all on the same side and this is some personal inner, office conflict," she said, thinking of some of her fellow officers and how much she didn't like them and vice versa.

Nonetheless, Maxwell's efforts to make her believe that her father and mother had been nothing more than vicious killers and terrorists had failed. This was because Romia was a cop, a good cop. Maxwell failed to realize she questioned everything and that his answers were weak and, therefore, she believed the opposite of all he'd told her. She believed the Phoenix had a bigger purpose than simply making trouble for the government. There had to be more to the story than what he presented.

Over the past few months, Romia had pondered the stories Maxwell had told her and some of the stories he'd told Royale. She'd stolen away time to research the names he dropped so carelessly. She found only the opposite to be true about her grandfather. She found that the man who had called himself the Phoenix was in fact a double agent—true—but the facts were, at least in her mind, that he was working to rid the world of those who had abused their power and authority. What looked like insanity was in fact genius misguided. The idea of finding a group of people with extraordinary abilities was like creating a bunch of comic book superheroes. Only the result wasn't what he had expected. There was no parade. There were no showers of confetti or congratulations. There was only angry, jealous people staring, pointing, and rejecting the "freaks" who stepped in to do what they themselves could not. Romia could relate to that.

Unorthodox were the Phoenix's ways, unconventional his undertaking, true, but Romia could see past that to his deeper mission. And, in her mind and heart, Maxwell was misleading her into believing that her grandfather was a bad person. It was unfortunate that she felt such a lack of trust in Maxwell, because for now she had to follow him. She had to follow him if for no other reason than to find her father. To find Stone would bring about clarity and that's what she sought now. She would let no one and nothing get in her way of seeking clarity. She needed it for herself and she promised it to Royale.

Royale didn't trust Maxwell either, and that was hard on him considering Maxwell had taken him and gave him what the nuns did not. But then again, Royale, too, was a puzzle of blurry lines. Nonetheless, Royale had earned her respect and friendship, which was hard to do. When they returned to Europe together, she and Royale would visit that convent and get to the bottom of his existence. There were secrets there at that convent and together they would find them.

"We could die in the dark, you know," Royale had said one night as they ran. They often ran at night, enjoying the silence of the air, filling it only with their breathing as they cleared mile after mile, strengthening themselves for a battle that Maxwell said was coming. The battle neither understood.

"Not me, I refuse to not understand this war."

"Then you agree we have been drafted."

"I have. I don't know about you. You seem content to serve."

"No. I'm not. I've only followed to see where this will end. I have only done what is required to find answers."

"You've killed to find answers to questions you don't even have?"

"Oh," Royale chuckled, turning and running backward after getting in front of her. "I have many questions. I'm just not openly inquisitive as you. I don't show my hands as easily as you."

"Are you saying that after all these years you've been with Maxwell you have not asked in the open what is his purpose?"

"Yes. His purpose is to find this man Stone and stop him from becoming as powerful as his father the Phoenix was."

"Hmm, I don't believe it. I believe it's more than that."

"What do you believe?" Royale asked.

"I believe you're expecting me to show my hand too easily," she said in French, showing that she'd been catching on quickly to the language. He laughed.

Yes, she believed Maxwell had an ulterior motive for wanting to find Stone, and once finding him, he would expose it.

And I believe he'll die at my father's hands, she thought suddenly as if realizing that thought for the first time. A shiver ran down her spin.

At that moment too, Keliegh moved slightly, causing Romia to jump. If he opened his eyes, she knew it would be too late to run, too late to hide.

"I can't let him see me," she mumbled. Her shame was more than she could handle. She didn't want him to look at her, to see her, not now, not after all the pain her life had caused him. Whether she understood any of the life she now lived, or not, it didn't matter; she was the reason poor Keliegh had suffered this way.

He had tried to save her from her destiny.

His eyes opened momentarily and locked on her for only a

second. His lips attempted to move but could not. She knew he assumed himself to be dreaming and if only he knew she was indeed standing there alive and well, surely he would have had mixed emotions.

"I love you, Keliegh," Romia said before touching his hand, making a connection, perhaps for the last time. "With more than all my heart."

At that moment, Keliegh nodded ever so slightly.

Had he heard her?

Romia knew it was time to go, but pulling away was the hardest thing she'd ever done in her life. Keliegh had been her first partner—in more ways than one.

She had no idea what lay ahead of her with this new group of people. They were the undead. That's what she'd come to call them as she had slowly begun to understand how they moved around in society, taking over lives of those who once lived. She didn't know yet if she trusted Olga and Jerry. They were following, but did they know where and why they were being led? What had he promised them?

Maybe they, too, were being blackmailed or coerced against their will. She'd need to find out more about her partners. There was nothing worse than trusting one's life to one who didn't care about his or her own.

None of it really mattered though. Romia was for right. Maybe she would rub off on them. Maybe she would make them question their allegiance to Maxwell . . . *maybe not.*

The transmitter in her watch beeped once. It was her signal to leave.

Royale had agreed to time her visit. "Since you have no brains where this man is concerned," he had barked, sounding jealous about her plans to visit Keliegh. He made no bones about his feelings where she and her feelings for Keliegh were concerned.

Stepping from the ICU unit as discreetly as she went in,

she made her way to the stairs. It always amazed her how unseen she could be while standing in the open. Dashing to the stairway, she used the railing to cover the several flights down within seconds. Reaching the fourth floor she disrobed, tossing the doctor's white jacket, surgical gloves, shoes, and paper booties, and the blonde wig in the trash. She then pulled off the slacks, and unrolled the skirt that she wore around her waist to bulk up her frame, and slipped into the flip-flops she had in tucked in the rolls of the skirt. She smoothed down the skirt before pulling up her natural hair into a bun and donning eye glasses and a fake beauty mark under her eye. She exited then through the bowels of the hospital.

Outside, Royale was waiting, right on time. He was dressed much like a college student today. Royale was never late when it came to meeting her, or connecting with her. It was as if she could read his mind and he hers. They seemed to move as one in thought. Even when he spoke in French she understood what he said. It was a strange sensation, true.

But nothing that compared to what she felt for Keliegh Jack.

Romia quickly climbed on the back of the motorcycle with Royale. They looked like two young people out for the day.

"Got him outta ya system?" he said over his shoulder.

"Never," Romia said, pulling the plain white helmet over her head, as he pulled off quickly.

Epilogue

It had been a year since Keliegh had found himself falling into and reopening the case of the mysterious group that called themselves the Phoenix team. Some around the precinct had implied they were a government agency, others implied they were terrorists. Whatever the case, they, in the end, had touched his life in ways he often did not want to talk about.

Tommy, too, was reluctant to review the past year. She'd healed from her injuries and had gone on with life with a fresh new vitality that spoke of a person who had grown from a traumatic or life-changing experience. She'd grown as a woman, allowing love to come in for Jim Beem—or—least a healthy amount of lust.

Maybe Keleigh had grown also or maybe not at all, for still he dreamed of the day in the hospital when he saw her beauty for the last time.

Was he dreaming?

"Of course I was," he mumbled aloud.

Nonetheless, perhaps it was best that everyone involved put this all behind them, as it was too difficult to really believe. The covert spy operation whose actual existence could not be proven to have existed. Spies counter spies, double agents, and ignominious acts of betrayal, murder, and borderline treason left Keliegh confused in his loyalties where the group was concerned. Were they good, or evil? Friend or foe? Was Romia real?

His mind went to the day she went up in flames. That was the hardest memory of all. The body recovered was confirmed to be her. Whatever pyro trick she thought she was playing didn't work.

"This poor girl didn't stand a chance of surviving this prank. I'll say it again, don't play with matches," Sam, in forensics, said. Normally those kinds of comments would have brought a joke or two, albeit in bad taste. But not that day. Tommy could barely hold it together long enough to get out of the room before giving way to tears. Thinking of her partner and how much losing Romia hurt, she couldn't help it.

Upon initial research, it was proven that Maxwell Huntington, the head of the IA, had been dead for many years. That information alone was enough to send Keliegh's mind into a tailspin back when he first heard it. However, it was the confirmation that, upon closer investigation, Romia Smith, as he knew her, never existed that had taken him over to the dark side, in his thoughts. The rest of the characters, as they played out this act, were inconsequential as far as he was concerned. They were just secondary actors in this wild fantasy performance.

How had Romia slipped into a life under the wire, and existed for thirty years as an upright and law-abiding woman? Was her life just a façade? Sometimes as he drove past her apartmetnt he would ask himself this question when tempted to stop and knock on the door.

What kind of mystic was she? Who was she really? What had she wanted? What had been her purpose and mission? Did she even know or was she an unwitting participant?

Keliegh would never be sure about Romia and her true loyalties. All he knew was that she wasn't who he thought she was, and that the woman she was had gone.

And maybe that was a good thing. He shook his head at that thought. No, that would never be a good thing. He tugged at his shirt in the area of his heart. No, losing Romia, or whoever she was, would never be a good thing.

Tonight, for the first time in a long time, Keliegh thought about all of it. Running it through his mind like a bad movie. The thoughts, each one, were tiring and laborious to get through. Stripping down to his shorts and climbing into bed, Keliegh gave into his mental and physical exhaustion. He'd healed completely from the physical injuries he'd incurred during the explosion and had been back to work for nearly a month.

Members of precinct overtly avoided the discussion of the incident surrounding Romia Smith. Even on Friday nights, hanging out at a new place in the Palemoes, ones who remembered Mike just let it go into the past. Truly it was a thing of the past. Even Lawrence and Jim never talked about it, although he was certain Jim had not let it go. Jim wasn't one to leave something unfinished. With Jim and Lawrence's beyond fair share of unusual cases on the books, Keliegh only hoped Jim would not get himself in trouble one day stepping too close to the mystery of the Phoenix.

Turning out the light, Keliegh lay on his back, noticing the full moon shining through his window as he finally gave into dozing.

Suddenly snapping awake, he felt the presence of someone in his room. Reaching for his gun he noticed the sensation passed as instantly as it came. "Shit," he gasped, sitting up in the bed. "I'm going nuts," he finally admitted.

Just then, as he reached for the small lamp, he felt a slender hand on his, stopping him from turning on the light. Grabbing hold of his interloper's wrist, he was blocked from any defense by the flat of a hand to his forehead, which knocked him back onto his pillow. Before he could rise up to fight he felt full lips covering his mouth. The kiss was warm, then hot, firm and then soft, before changing to one more desperate and hungry.

He was confused, yet highly affected as his tongue played in a frighteningly familiar volley. Reaching for the visitor's head, he felt the long hair which fell freely, stroking his face. Pulling from the kiss, he tried to adjust his eyes, but was given no time as the woman mounted him, sliding down on his manhood which stood erect and ready, exposed through the front of his undershorts. He was ready to penetrate her, which she allowed, seething in instant pleasure, squirming and riding him as if he were her possession. Keliegh groaned in pleasure, allowing the violation. He bit her neck and her breasts as the two of them groped and wrestled in a lover's battle for sweet conquest.

Panting and gasping, the woman climaxed, yet did not tire or show a break in her hunger for him. Pulling his shoulder, she rolled over, pulling him on her where he then took the advantage position, sliding into the beauty whose face was still not well defined. Her entire body was black as the dark room around them. She was no more than a . . . *shadow* . . . against his bed sheets.

Maybe this was a dream; he would only imagine it to be, as nothing real could be this fantastic, this genuinely wonderful.

"Who are you?" he asked, rising up into a push-up position while going deep into her pleasure. "Who . . ." Again his inquiry was interrupted by her eager lips, mouth, and tongue as she pulled him down to her. She grabbed at his ears, urging his stroke to quicken by arching upward.

Her thighs were taunt, her arms muscular, her scent familiar.

Within moments he exploded inside her and together their breathing bated and undulated, until eventually he slid from her tightness and fell over to the side of her.

In the darkened room, his mouth opened as he voiced the impossible question. "Romia?" he asked her.

The woman was still for the first time since he became aware of her presence. Suddenly rising up, she hovered over him. It may have been his imagination, but her eyes were clearly seen for the first time tonight. That is before, with a short, quick movement of her hand to the side of his head, she rendered him unconscious.

"Sleep well, my love," she said. "I shall visit you again one day," she promised.

"So are you happy now?" Royale asked, surprising her with his presence.

Again he'd followed her, found her, seemingly knowing her next move. She'd parked over five blocks away and in the darkness of the night she'd run back to her motorcycle that waited for her. Reaching the bike, she stopped abruptly at the sight of Royale leaning against the building dressed in his normal black attire. Only tonight he wore no mask. He looked like a normal young man just out for an evening ride. She smiled broadly, unable to hold on to her formally tight expression. She smiled a lot these days and with good reason. The trip to the convent had revealed to them both many secrets that changed their lives in a good way.

"Very," she answered, pulling on the skull cap she had in her pocket and then sliding her helmet onto her head. She mounted her motorcycle.

Royale mounted his, parked next to hers, as well. Before sliding his helmet over his woolly locks, he grinned without looking at her directly.

Together they drove off toward the direction of the rising sun.

Notes

Notes

Notes

ORDER FORM
URBAN BOOKS, LLC
78 E. Industry Ct
Deer Park, NY 11729

Name: (please print):_____

Address: _____

City/State: _____

Zip: _____

QTY	TITLES	PRICE
	The Cartel	$14.95
	The Cartel#2	$14.95
	The Dopeman's Wife	$14.95
	The Prada Plan	$14.95
	Gunz And Roses	$14.95
	Snow White	$14.95
	A Pimp's Life	$14.95
	Hush	$14.95
	Little Black Girl Lost 1	$14.95
	Little Black Girl Lost 2	$14.95
	Little Black Girl Lost 3	$14.95
	Little Black Girl Lost 4	$14.95

Shipping and handling - add $3.50 for 1st book, then $1.75 for each additional book.

Please send a check payable to:

Urban Books, LLC

Please allow 4 - 6 weeks for delivery

ORDER FORM
URBAN BOOKS, LLC
78 E. Industry Ct
Deer Park, NY 11729

Name: (please print):_____

Address: _____

City/State: _____

Zip: _____

QTY	TITLES	PRICE
	16 ½ On The Block	$14.95
	16 On The Block	$14.95
	Betrayal	$14.95
	Both Sides Of The Fence	$14.95
	Cheesecake And Teardrops	$14.95
	Denim Diaries	$14.95
	Happily Ever Now	$14.95
	Hell Has No Fury	$14.95
	If It Isn't love	$14.95
	Last Breath	$14.95
	Loving Dasia	$14.95
	Say It Ain't So	$14.95

Shipping and handling - add $3.50 for 1st book, then $1.75 for each additional book.
Please send a check payable to:
    Urban Books, LLC
Please allow 4 - 6 weeks for delivery

ORDER FORM
URBAN BOOKS, LLC
78 E. Industry Ct
Deer Park, NY 11729

Name: (please print):_____

Address: _____

City/State: _____

Zip: _____

QTY	TITLES	PRICE
	A Man's Worth	$14.95
	Abundant Rain	$14.95
	Battle Of Jericho	$14.95
	By The Grace Of God	$14.95
	Dance Into Destiny	$14.95
	Divorcing The Devil	$14.95
	Forsaken	$14.95
	Grace And Mercy	$14.95
	Guilty & Not Guilty Of Love	$14.95
	His Woman, His Wife His Widow	$14.95
	Illusions	$14.95
	The LoveChild	$14.95

Shipping and handling - add $3.50 for 1st book, then $1.75 for each additional book.
Please send a check payable to:
    Urban Books, LLC
Please allow 4 - 6 weeks for delivery

ORDER FORM
URBAN BOOKS, LLC
78 E. Industry Ct
Deer Park, NY 11729

Name: (please print):_____

Address: _____

City/State: _____

Zip: _____

QTY	TITLES	PRICE

Shipping and handling - add $3.50 for 1st book, then $1.75 for each additional book.
Please send a check payable to:
    Urban Books, LLC
Please allow 4 - 6 weeks for delivery